I0622322

Published by Jet Black Ink

First printing

© Copyright 2014-All Rights Reserved

LIBRARY OF CONGRESS CATALOGING-IN-PUBLICATION DATA

Stunt/Jet Black

ISBN-13: 978-0692354308
ISBN-10: 0692354301

LCCN: 2014959987

1. Erotica-Fiction. 2. Relationships-Fiction.
3. Romance-Fiction. 4. Mystery-Fiction.

Printed in the United States of America

STUNT

JET BLACK

Prologue

"Well anyway," she said. "I know you're eager and all, but the best I can do is get you on the set as a stunt dick."

"A stunt dick? What the hell is a stunt dick?" I asked.

She laughed, stood up and took off her baseball cap, revealing more of that fascinating long, curly, red hair. "Oh, you *are* new to all of this, aren't you? How cute." I leaned forward, eager to hear her answer. "You know how a stunt man fills in and does all the fighting and breaking through glass and jumping off tall buildings for the high-paid actors in the movies?"

I nodded. "Yeah?"

"Okay. So a stunt dick fills in for the star when he can't get it up or if he can't come or if we need a big money shot and the star has no load."

Chapter 1

The last time Denise and I made love, we did it like porn stars. It started with a text at three o'clock in the afternoon the first Friday in August.

Hurry home babe. Been playing w/my favorite toy and I am SO wet. I need the real thing.

The words transformed my iPhone to Viagra in an instant. I hit REPLY.

I'm gonna beat it up so bad, you ain't gonna be able to walk all weekend.

I started to grab my dick, but then I heard a knock on my office door. "Come in," I said. Theresa, our office manager, opened it and stuck her face in.

"They're ready for you in the main conference room," she said. Then she smiled. She'd been with my little telemarketing start-up, The Phone Room, for two years now and she had been dieting 23 out of those 24 months.

"Thanks Theresa," I said half thinking about the meeting and half thinking about the boner stretching out my Dockers courtesy of the text. "Tell 'em I'll be right there."

Jet Black

"No problem Mr. Stunt," she said before her head disappeared. I listened to her stride clickity-clop down the hardwood hallway before I stood, adjusted my rod, and prepared myself for the meeting with my two partners and our small staff.

I'll wear something sexy.

Just thinking about Denise's smooth, tan skin, her fragrant blonde hair, that sexy little Pilate-doing body made me want to blow off the meeting and let my partners handle it. After all, what good is it to be an owner if you can't sneak off early every now and then?

I knew better than that though. When I started this company, I worked longer hours than I ever did in my thirty years on this earth. This included my time spent in the Air Force, working double and sometimes, alternate shifts. Plus, being the only black partner, I wasn't about to let anybody stereotype me as being lazy.

Keep it wet for me baby.

I sent Denise the text and turned off my phone.

The meeting dragged. It was about new clients visiting, losing a small client and sales figures. Don't get me wrong, I was grateful for those clients,

2

the sales and for having my own, but now it was the end of the week and my mind was only on one thing.

I zoomed my 750i up I-85. The clock on the dash read 4:35. I knew if I hurried, I could beat the Atlanta rush-hour traffic that made you want to kill somebody if you got stuck in it. With the help of an energy drink and some serious House music on satellite radio, I was parked in front of our condo in record time.

I checked my mini-fro in the rearview mirror, popped in a piece of gum, and sprayed a little bit of the expensive cologne she'd bought me on my shirt. Just then, I caught a glimpse of Denise's eyes peeping through a bent down blind. I loved it when she did that because I knew she couldn't wait for it. The big hand in my pants went from six to midnight.

`I need the real thing.`

And the real thing needed her.

When I opened the front door, the aroma of vanilla scented candles made my nose happy while the sound of the CD titled Porn's Greatest Hits Volume One bow-chicky-bow-wowwed through the stereo speakers. And lickety-split, she appeared out of nowhere like a blur of hair and bare nipples. She'd already leaped into my arms and was working her tongue down my throat like she wanted my piece of Orbitz all to herself. Oh, she wanted a piece all right, but it sure as hell wasn't any gum.

As I carried her from the foyer to the sofa, lips still locked, I laid her down and finally got a glimpse of what she was barely wearing.

"What took you so long?" she asked. That cute little half-grin of hers gave me chills. Then she bit her bottom lip.

"Another long meeting," I said. But after seeing her in something that looked like a red nursing bra with the middle flaps cut out and a pair of matching, lace panties, the only meeting I cared about was the one between her body and mine.

Denise sat up, fumbled with my belt buckle, undid the button, the zipper, and let the pants fall to the floor.

"Holy shit Ricky," she said into my briefs like they were a microphone. Did you get even *bigger* since last night?" She kissed on my stomach and removed my Hanes nice and slow.

I'd planned on saying something clever like 'Baby, my shit is like a Chia Pet, it keeps growing and growing and growing." But when her mouth worked its magic on my Johnson, all I managed was, "Baby my shooooooooweeee!"

Had it not been for the kegels I did daily, I would have exploded right then and there. Instead, I eased her back down on the couch and sucked on her juicy double-dees like my life depended on them.

"Oh Ricky," she said and then put her arms around me. As she stroked my back, I felt the metal of her engagement ring on my bare skin. Whenever she touched me, it was like electricity flowing through my body.

I kissed her bellybutton, sucked on her belly, and let my fingers play with the diamond piercing in the middle. "I love it when you do that," She said and I smiled. I continued to work my way down and kissed the warmth and wetness from outside of her panties before removing them on either side with my hands. I was on my way to taste her sweet saltiness when she pushed my head and said, "Uh uh babe. I've been waiting too long. You'd better put that big, black, eight inch cock in me right now or so help me I'll scream."

I kneeled over her, grabbed it with my hand and said, "Oh, this is what you want huh?"

"Stop playing Ricky!" We laughed together. "You know I've been waiting all day."

"Can a brother at least get his shirt off?"

"No."

"Well in that case, your wish is my command."

I ain't one to brag, but ever since I started boning, I never had a problem pleasing the ladies. In high school, girls whose cherries I'd popped only ended up crying over me when I told them I wasn't ready for a relationship. In my military days, I had them oohing and aahing from Texas to Turkey, from Oslo to Ohio. So by the time I met Denise, I had so much between-the-sheets know-how that I could have made it as a gigolo. Of course, being hung like a mule don't hurt none either.

When I put it in, I watched her face change from happy to ecstatic. And if you don't know the difference, you ain't doing it right.

She grabbed my ass and pulled me in even more, letting out a loud "yes," here, an "ooh," and "ahh," there.

A faster song started on the CD and I stroked faster right along with the beat. This lasted a good ten minutes or so.

"You wanna ride the pony?" I said. She opened her eyes and took a short break from euphoria.

"Mmm hmm," she said. And when she was up there, it was like a dream. While she rode me, she touched me, touched it with her hand. When she bent down to kiss me, her hair covered my face and the sweet smell of fresh flowers engulfed me.

When I sat up, I kissed her breasts, sucked the nipples, placed them between my finger and thumb and rubbed. I went back and forth. Forth and back. Mouth. Hands. Tongue. Fingers.

She leaned her head back and started to move faster. Up and down. Harder. "You like that steel dick inside of you?"

"Oh god. Your dick is like magic!" Her face was flush now. She had that familiar look on her face and I knew what was next. Those four little words. Shakita screamed them in the back of my Impala parked in my high school's parking lot. Mary Sue sang them with a country twang on her bed in San Antonio the day after my military training. And Andari "ah kee keeed!!!" it in a hotel in Turkey just outside Incirlik Air Force base. "I'm about to cuuuuuuuuuuuuuuuuummmmmmmmmmm!"

When she was done drowning out the music and giving the neighbors something to talk about, she got down on all fours on the floor and said, "Don't leave me down here all by myself."

I couldn't help but grin because she knew exactly what I liked and how I liked it. It didn't take long for me to not only join her on the floor but adjoin to her from behind like a puzzle piece.

As I pumped in and out, each time harder and faster, my hands had a mind of their own. I grabbed her waist, her bodacious tah tahs, and my hands even made their way to her mouth where she sucked and licked on each finger like Kentucky Fried Chicken.

"I've been a bad girl," she said as she rose up and grabbed my thighs from behind.

"Oh yeah?" I said. "Guess you need a good spankin' huh?"

"Uh huh."

I gave her a couple or three or four of good smacks and that's when it all came together like some beautiful symphony. The sound of her oohs, and fuck mes, and yeses over the bow chicky wow wow music. The smell of her hair and the vanilla in the air and the sweet smell of funky lovemaking. The feel of her hands rubbing my thighs, cupping my balls. And the urge to try to make it last forever like my name was Keith Sweat, knowing goddamn well I was about to explode inside of her like a grenade in a shoebox. "I'm gonna cuuummm!"

I never did get my shirt off that night. I woke up ten hours later on the floor with her head lying on my chest. It had been one of the best nights of my life.

Chapter 2

Three days later, Denise's body was found on the shores of Lake Lanier and my world turned to shit. It was a hot Monday night in August, and I figured she must have been running late coming home from work. Sometimes at the studio they could go hours into the night, making sure each scene was shot just right, each soundtrack fit the scene, and all the actors got their fair share of camera time.

Sometimes she wouldn't make it in until after midnight because the director needed her help in making every scene look perfect. Or he needed her to coach some newbie into making a scene look more realistic.

When I heard a knock at the door around 9:30, my heart hit my stomach. Call it a hunch, intuition, or instincts from my Office of Special Investigations days in the Air Force. Whatever it was, I knew it was bad.

I grabbed the remote, pressed POWER, and turned off the talking heads on ESPN. A look through the peephole verified my hunch. There stood two Atlanta police officers; their cruiser parked on the street. I unlocked the dead bolt and opened the door.

"Good evening sir. Are you Mr. Richard Stunt?" One cop asked. He was shaved bald and pitch black, like he'd played in the hot Georgia sun all of his life. Dressed in a dark blue uniform, he held his hat in his hand as he waited for my reply.

"I go by Ricky. What's going on?" I feared the worst.

"May we come in?" asked the other officer, a white guy with a crew cut that reminded me of the service. He had a Southern accent that for some reason made me think of movies about the Klan and lynching.

"Of course," I said. I motioned for them to come in and then I shut the door. They stood in the foyer.

"I'm sorry to have to tell you this," the black cop said as I felt my knees buckle. "But a Miss Denise Dupont was found dead..." My heart raced and I began to feel dizzy. The officer was still talking but the words all became mish-mash to me. My mouth got dry like I was in the Sahara Desert. My knees were like Weeble Wobbles, and my head was a spinning top. I needed the sofa.

"Are you okay sir?" the white officer said.

"I need to sit down." I couldn't focus. I felt my way to the couch like a blind man and plopped down, half sitting, half lying. I wanted to go to sleep right there and wake up from this nightmare.

"Should we call the paramedics?" the white officer asked before sitting next to me. His shiny nametag read Sawyer in black letters.

"Can I get you some water?" said the other officer. But I had enough water filling up my eyes to cry a river.

"No, uh, no thank you. Please. Just tell me what happened?"

"I'm sorry Mr. Stunt. It's still an ongoing investigation. We don't have a lot of information right now. All we know is her body was found at Lake Lanier. We found an insurance card in her wallet that listed you as the person to contact in case of an emergency. And her driver's license had this address." He surveyed the living room like he was looking for clues. "I take it she was your girlfriend?"

"Fiancé. We were getting married New Year's Eve."

"Do you know of anyone who would want to harm her?" Sawyer asked.

"No." The officers gave each other a look as if they weren't satisfied with the answer.

"And how were things at home?" the black officer asked. I squinted to get a look at his nametag and it read Jackson.

"Fine. I told you we were getting married."

"Did she have any relatives in the area?" Sawyer asked. It pissed me off that they were speaking of her in past tense like she'd been gone for years instead of hours.

"Her mother passed away, and her father hasn't been in touch for years. She has an aunt in Nebraska that she's close with. That's about it."

"I see," said Sawyer. He stood and readied himself to leave. "Well, Mr. Stunt. We are truly sorry for your loss. If you think of anything, please call us."

Jackson reached into his front shirt pocket, pulled out a business card and handed it to me.

"Yes. We're sorry for your loss," he echoed.

"Thank you officers." I stood to walk them to the door. When I opened it, I could see a few nosey neighbors whispering, probably trying to figure out what the problem was. After all, this was a quiet neighborhood.

"If you could come down to the station, whenever you're up to it, maybe you can speak with one of our detectives. Help 'em figure some things out," said Sawyer.

"Yeah," Jackson finished. "Anything you can think of that can help us find the party responsible for this would be greatly appreciated."

"Of course," I said as I shut the door.

As I sat in the living room, the reality of Denise's death hit me hard. I clenched my teeth because I wasn't going to give the bastard who did that to her the satisfaction of making me cry. Every little thing now reminded me of her. The snapshots of our vacation in Venice sitting in the gondola. The sofa and loveseat that she had to have when we stopped at Ethan Allen to look for something to replace my futon when she moved in. Even the dining room table, where I sat and blew out the candles on my cake she got for me for my 30th birthday. To top it off, we'd made love in all those places, on all those places.

   I promised myself I wouldn't rest until I got the motherfucker that killed my woman.

Chapter 3

Tuesday morning, I wanted to choke the shit out of the newspaper reporter responsible for the headline:

EX-PORN STAR FOUND DEAD AT LAKE LANIER

I had made up my mind that I was going to sue the shit out of the Atlanta Journal Constitution or handle this shit with some gasoline and a match. My baby deserved better than that.

I couldn't even read the whole article. Just the part about Denise Dupont...AKA Double-D Dee...found dead...age 28...former adult film star...blah blah blah...foul play suspected....No suspects.

"No suspects my ass," I said out loud. Then I thought about what Jackson and Sawyer said about me coming down to the station. Fuck that. Those motherfuckers had no suspects. I wasn't about to go down there for a so-called interview and become prime suspect number one. They'd pin that shit on me and claim some domestic violence bullshit. I could see that detective now just looking at my six feet tall, athletic-looking ass and having O.J. flashbacks. They couldn't solve a crime if it bit 'em in the ass. There was only one brother who had the smarts, the balls, and who really gave a damn enough to solve Denise's murder. And that person was me, Ricky Stunt.

I made myself a big pot of coffee because caffeine helped me to think. Then I called one of my partners at the firm, Mike Moore. I'd known Mike since we'd worked together a few years ago. He was the coolest white dude I knew. Mike used to hang with me at all the Hip Hop and R & B clubs. Back then, everybody called him White Mike. We looked odd together with him standing at only 5 foot 3 and a face kind of like Marky Mark and me with my six foot frame and looking like a GQ model. That was before he got married and had a kid and before me and Denise got serious.

I remember the time at Club XO; I opened up to him about why I'd left the military. The drinks were flowing and so was my mouth.

"How does a decorated war veteran end up taking a job as a telemarketer anyway?" Mike asked.

"The Air Force said I didn't always play by the rules."

"What did you do, fuck some colonel's wife?"

"No but I got fucked by a colonel at my court martial. Full-bird, I-know-the UCMJ-by-heart motherfucker. Colonel Stewart Banks. I'll never forget that name. Said my interrogation techniques were causing too many suspects to end up crippled or dead. I guess they were in need of more kinder, gentler military."

"What about your degree?"

"The degree don't mean shit when your DD214 says Dishonorable Discharge. The only job I could find that didn't need a thorough background check was the telemarketing gig. I had to start my life all over again. Luckily, I had some money saved up. At least he didn't send me to Leavenworth to get pounded in the ass."

"Well, they say everything happens for a reason," he said. Then he downed his shot.

"That's true. I guess I wouldn't have even considered this profession if I had gotten a job as a cop or something. Then I ended up learning the business and starting my own."

Not to mention meeting Denise.

"So what ever happened to that colonel?"

"Fuck if I know," I said before downing another shot of tequila. "It's not like we're Facebook friends or anything. Last I heard, he was working on his third star in Europe somewhere."

I had the idea to start my own telemarketing firm. I wrote out the business plan on a napkin and shared it with him.

"Do you need a partner?" he said. "I've been saving up some money to do my own thing too." Truth was, I could use a couple of partners. My dream was big and it needed bright people with their own cash to add to mine. So we brought in Ari Levi as our chief financial officer. Ari was a by-the-book kind of guy, which was just what we needed to stay focused and realize our dream.

Even though I was kind of tight with Mike, I never told him or anybody else I work with about my personal life. That included Denise, her past, and our engagement. Plus, who could relate to a man falling for an ex-porn star anyway?

I picked up my iPhone and dialed Mike's cell.

"Hey Ricky. What's up?"

I exhaled and looked at a picture of my fiancé. "Hey Mike. I'm gonna need to take some time off. I had a death in the family."

"Oh no. I'm sorry to hear that man." I could hear his toddler daughter in the background laughing and screaming. "How can I help?"

"If you and Ari can just hold down the fort for a couple of weeks while I get myself together, that would be really great."

"Do you want to postpone the meeting with Moblicity? I know that's your baby."

No, Denise was my baby, I thought. "No. I know you can handle it. I'll e-mail you my notes and the PowerPoint."

"All right buddy. Things won't be the same without you. My condolences man."

"Thanks. I'll see you in a couple of weeks. Bye."

I knew Mike would come through for me. He respected my privacy and knew not to ask for too many details. He was a good friend and a great business partner. There were some days I wanted to tell him about Denise, but I decided to continue keeping my work life and home life separate.

Now that I knew work was taken care of, I could focus on Denise. First, I had to take care of her final arrangements. But after that, it would be time for revenge.

Chapter 4

We had a small, gravesite ceremony for Denise. The heat shattered records that day but that wasn't the only thing making me hot. Since we pretty much kept to ourselves, I didn't get a chance to meet a lot of her family and friends. I had grabbed her cell and dialed every number except the ones labeled WORK and my own to tell them of the news and to find out how they knew her.

The result was a dismal, 28 attendees, one for each year of her life. This included her aunt Martha from Nebraska, some of her friends from high school and beauty school, and a couple of our neighbors who'd loaned us a cup of sugar every now and then or told us the details about the last condo association meeting we couldn't attend.

It was no shock when I asked Aunt Martha about Denise's dad.

"He disowned her years ago when she decided to live by her own rules," she said of her brother. "I called him, but he said he wanted no part of her, even in death."

No one from her job was there and my gut was telling me somebody at that studio knew what happened that night at the lake. I was ready to get to the bottom of it.

The following Thursday, I rented a little black
Chevy Cobalt and made my way to the studio in
Atlantic Station. I'd only been to the building a few
times, like when Denise had car trouble or when she
had her pupils dilated and needed me to drive her.
Still, I didn't want to take any chances of anyone
recognizing me, so I left my BMW in the driveway
at home.

When I was finally up close to the building that
read Excelsior Modeling Agency, I imagined it
imploding like they sometimes show on the news. I
wanted everything in that building to die. *Yeah,
right. Modeling agency my ass.* Either the cops were
too stupid to see this was a front for making skin
flicks or somebody down there was getting a piece
of the action. *Who needs a front for porn anyway? I
thought that shit was legal.*

I walked through the glass double doors
wearing a simple but well-fitted blue Polo shirt,
some black khakis, and a pair of Kenneth Cole
shoes. My afro had been freshly trimmed and the
shower gel I used earlier still made my skin smell
good.

The lobby was nice. There were a few purple
couches and chairs. Bright lights. A fountain.
Linoleum floors. And photos of women and men
who looked like they belonged in a Calvin Klein ad.
To my left there were three men completing
paperwork on a clipboard. They were built like

cornerbacks in the NFL. There was an older woman seated next to them with her teenage daughters. They couldn't have been older than 14 and 15. Should have been home watching Hannah Montana instead trying to become models at such an early age.

I saw two tall and gorgeous women, one black and one Puerto Rican, gripping cases that looked like portfolios approach the receptionist. I got closer and listened.

"Hello. I'm Alicia Renee."

"And I'm Rosaria," she said rolling the Rs like smoking papers. "We'd like to show Excelsior our portfolios."

The receptionist, a redbone with a bit of meat on her bones, stood up. If I had to guess, I'd say she was about five five and near 40. She was kind of cute. Looked like she might have already popped out a few kids but not quite ready for granny drawers. Though the six foot something models dwarfed her, it was obvious who was in control.

"I'm sorry ladies," she said. "We're not looking for new talent at this time." As I checked out the behinds of one Alicia and one Rosaria, Miss Receptionist was burning a hole in my khakis, then my chest, then my khakis again like she'd been hypnotized. When she finally looked me in the eye, I'd noticed that her whole demeanor had changed.

She went from security guard to horny ho in the blink of an eye.

"Well hello," she said while tugging on one of her earrings. "Are you here to audition for the part?"

I wrinkled my forehead and said, "No, but I'd like to ask you a few questions if you don't mind."

In a snap, the security guard was back. "Oh, I'm sorry. I don't do questions. Next." She dismissed me like the school had bell rang.

One of the men who had been holding a clipboard was standing right behind me.

"Excuse me brother," he said.

As I turned to walk away, I glanced back at the receptionist and her eyes were trying to melt the seat off my pants.

I was almost through the glass doors when it hit me. If I was going to find out what happened to Denise, I would have to play by a different set of rules.

Instead of leaving, I sat on one of those couches that looked like Prince had designed it and waited until the lobby was clear. After ten minutes or so, I went back to the receptionist.

"You again?" she asked before crossing her arms over her chest. "I told you, I don't do questions."

"No, no, no," I said raising my hands. "I think you misunderstood me. It's just that I'm new to this and I was feeling a little insecure about letting you know I'm here to audition. I've never done anything like this before."

You would have thought I told her she had just won the Georgia Lottery because she cheesed like her picture was being taken.

"Oh. Well, why didn't you say so," she said. Now she was stroking her hair. She went to find me a clipboard and a form but fumbled it all like she had butter on her fingers. *There's my horny little ho*, I thought.

"What's your name miss?"

"It's Karen."

"Karen. I was wondering." I looked around as if searching for eavesdroppers. "Is there anywhere around here we could go to talk about how I might fast track my way in front of a director?"

I could almost see Karen's mind calculating. The A/C was blazing, but I could see beads of sweat bubbling on her forehead.

"Hmmm. I am due for my break right about now. Why don't I show you to the cloak room?"

"As long as it's private."

Karen grabbed her purse, put up a BACK IN 30 MINUTES sign, and led me down a hallway to the cloak room. As I walked behind her I thought, *I can't believe I'm about to do this*.

Karen shut the door to the cloak room. It was dark but the light from the sun shone through. From that point she was all hands. Eh, maybe a little bit of tongue, but definitely all hands. When she yanked at my shirt like a lawnmower cord, a button flew off and popped her straight in the forehead. I held back a laugh and decided to remove my own shirt before she caused any more damage.

"You have a great body," she said. Then she started to kiss my pecks. "You could be a star in this industry."

I played the role. Pretended I wanted her. I smooched on her neck while I undid the buttons and zippers on her business skirt. Freak wasn't even wearing any panties. "I showed you mine. Now show me yours."

I pulled down my pants and drawers at the same time and showed her mine all right. Her eyes got wide like she was at the casino and just saw three cherries. I knew goddamn well I wasn't about to bust no cherry. "Dayuuuum!" she said. She reached in her purse, pulled out a condom and rolled it over my anaconda so fast there might be a spot for her in the Guinness Book of World Records.

Fucking in a closet is like living in a Pinto. Just because it can be done doesn't mean it's a good idea to do it.

Karen leaned back against the wall. I gripped her plump ass on the sides before entering her from the front.

"Oh my god!" she screamed. She was loud like the finale on the 4th of July. I don't think she gave a damn about who heard us either. Or maybe she just couldn't control herself. I've been known to have that effect on women.

"Take this dick girl," I said through my teeth. I would have said her name if I remembered it. "Yeah. Take it all." I braced myself on the wall behind her.

It didn't take long for her to get to those four magic words. It was the other three that caught me off guard. "Come with me."

What the hell? Do I look like a synchronized swimmer? Is this a duet like Endless Love and my ass became Lionel Richie?

And just when I was about to tell her, "It's all about you" or "Do you" or "Get your own rocks off first," she was already singing soprano and my praises at the same time.

When her body stopped jerking, she asked, "Is there anything I can do for you?"

Truth is, I didn't even want to bust a nut. But somehow, I had the feeling that she was the kind of chick whose ego would deflate if she didn't make me come. "I'll take a blow job."

When she was down there on her knees, taking me in and out of her mouth like she was bobbing for apples, I reached up and grabbed a hold of a coat rod. Then she started using her hand with her mouth, stroking, sucking, sucking, and stroking. She even cupped my balls. And when I told her "I'm about to come," she said, "not in my mouth." But now the faucet was on and it was just a matter of time before the hot water came gushing. I borrowed a button-down shirt I had found on a hanger, pushed her head out of the way, starched the shit out of that shirt and grunted like a caveman.

"Money shot," she sang like she was proud of herself. Frickin' cougar.

I finished cleaning myself off with that poor dude's shirt and wished I could have seen the expression on his face when he came to retrieve it.

"So about that director," I said while pulling up my pants and briefs.

"Right," she said. Her hand disappeared into her purse. When it appeared again, it revealed a white business card. "This is my good friend Melissa's card. Melissa Summers. She's the lighting director for most of the films we do here. Give her a call tomorrow and tell her Karen sent you.

I took the card and put on my shirt. The two of us tried to smooth out our wrinkled clothes, fix our hair, and wipe off the sweat.

I opened the closet door and we made our way to the lobby. When we got back to her desk I asked, "So am I gonna get fast tracked past those other guys I saw in the lobby today?"

Stunt

"Oh honey," she said. "With your skills, that body, and a word from Melissa, you might be starring in your own films before they even get a chance to audition."

"Cool," I said. I made my way to the door. "It's been fun."

"Wait. wait. I didn't even catch your name."
That's how hoes do it.

"Ricky Stunt," I said then I pimp-walked out the door into the sweet, Atlanta sunshine.

Just like I'd read her, Karen was a hoe. But if I was going to solve Denise's murder, I knew I was going to have to deal with people just like her and get my hands and my balls dirty. I was going to have to use everything I knew and everything I had in order to figure this thing out, even if I had to screw my way to the top.

Chapter 5

The next morning, I plopped down at the kitchen counter at home and worked that coffee down my throat like Karen worked me down hers yesterday. Even though Denise was gone, it felt like I had just cheated on her. When I made it home last night, I hit the shower hard, scrubbing every crevice, getting the smell of cougar juice off me. I'd almost forgotten what it was like to have sex without love, to make my body numb and take my mind elsewhere.

After my shower, I took out a notepad and started writing down clues, evidence, and revelations like I'd learned in the Office of Special Investigations. I wanted to head down to the lake and look for evidence. But knowing how the cops work, they would have been there too. Probably would have said I was returning to the scene of the crime.

I started to feel like I was back in Iraq investigating local terrorists or at Wright-Patterson weeding out our own troops selling secrets to the enemy. Just then, I recalled a conversation I had at dinner when Denise first told me her secret.

We were having dinner at Justin's. Everything was perfect. Fresh lobster in the tank at the entrance. White linen table cloths. Sparkling chandeliers. A friendly waitress and efficient busboy who kept our water glasses filled.

This was our fifth date and things were getting serious. Denise held my hand, looked into my eyes, and got it off her chest.

"There's something I need to tell you."

"Okay."

"It's about my past."

"Go on," I said. The waitress placed my surf and turf on the table, then Denise's grilled salmon and rice. We thanked her.

"Do you need anything else?" She was a cute brunette.

"You need anything, baby?" I asked Denise. She shook her head. I gave the waitress a brief smile. "No. Everything is perfect. Thank you."

"Okay. I'll be here if you need me," she said. Then she disappeared into the kitchen. I was going to give her a big tip.

"You were saying?" I asked. I unfolded my napkin and placed it on my lap. Denise did the same.

"I don't quite know how to tell you this."

"It's okay," I assured her and held her hands tight. "Just say it."

"I used to be an adult film actress," she said.

My eyes bulged and my mind raced with thoughts of orgies, girl-on-girl, AIDS, happy endings, and money shots. I grabbed my ice water and downed it like I'd just run a 5K. A piece of ice got stuck in my throat. I choked and coughed hard two or three times.

The busboy, an Asian guy who reminded me of Brandon Lee, appeared out of nowhere and refilled my glass. He was gone just as fast. Probably would have given me the Heimlich if I needed it.

"Are you okay Ricky?"

My body was. But the bombshell she'd dropped on me caused temporary damage to my psyche.

"Yeah," I said. "Just a little ice in my throat. I'm okay. Why did you wait until now to tell me?"

"I had to know for sure I was falling in love with you. When we met at that networking event, I was already done making my last film. That's the reason I was there, to look into a new career altogether."

"You told me you worked for a modeling agency. Was that a lie?" My hands retreated under the table and I was looking around to see who was within earshot.

"The thing is, the modeling agency is kind of a front for a little film company, Buck Nekkid Productions. And here's the kicker. Don't kill me, but I still work there, but only behind the scenes now. I promise."

I was speechless. I carved a piece of turf and shoved it in my mouth. I chewed and thought of the next thing to say. I was falling in love with her too. And that was challenging enough with her being white and me being, um, not. Now, I started to wonder if the stares we got were more than about race. Maybe somebody recognized her. That dude who'd parked the car. That chick driving the pickup truck with the confederate flag license plates. That sista who'd rolled her eyes.

What I said was, "How many flicks we talkin' about here?" What I was thinking was, *How many dicks we talkin' about here?*

"Just five or six. I knew it wasn't for me when I sampled that world. Between the cattiness, the nastiness, and the behind-the-scenes grit of the business, I knew I had to do something else," she said.

"So why not leave it all together? Make a clean break?"

"Believe me, I'm gonna. But this economy is crazy and there isn't a lot of work for ex-porn stars with a year of beauty school under their belts. Plus, it's not easy to replace that kind of money. This director, Monte, took pity on me and told me he needed a production assistant to help him out. Do hair and make-up, that kind of stuff. And since I went to beauty school, it was a perfect fit. I've been saving my money to start my own hair and make-up business."

As least she has a plan, I thought. "And this is legit? You don't have to blow this Monte guy or anything do you?" I asked.

"Hell no. He's happily married with kids. And his wife is beautiful. Much too good for his bald ass."

"I thought Hollywood was the place to make adult films."

"It was, ten years ago. But now with the internet, and web cams, and Skype, you can pretty much make a porno anywhere. There's this girl in Lincoln who lives a mile from my aunt Martha. She makes a killing just doing web shows, selling subscriptions to any loser with a credit card." She flashed me her million dollar smile as I shoveled rice into my mouth.

If this had been any other woman, I might have stood up, paid the check, and walked out forever. But Denise was special. And it wasn't about the sex. She had a way of drawing you in and engaging you. A way of making you feel like you're the only person in a crowded room. Call me a fool if you want, but I was falling in love with Miss Denise Dupont. And some bullshit from her past wasn't about to change our future.

"Any more questions?"

"Just one," I said. "What was your adult film name?"

"Double D-Dee."

I cracked up like Cedric the Entertainer was doing stand-up beside us. And when I did, she couldn't help but crack a smile too.

"So you're okay with this?" she asked. That was the $100,000 question.

"You don't see me leaving do you?"

Chapter 6

I reviewed my notes but didn't have much to go on. Denise's cell only had one number in her contacts listed as WORK and when I dialed it Karen answered. I pressed END when I heard her voice. The only texts she had were from me and the last one read:

Keep it wet for me baby.

All I had was names. Karen, Monte, and Melissa Summers. I remembered how she used to talk about the long hours she put in and how Monte was such a perfectionist.

I went to my laptop and Googled Monte and Buck Nekkid Productions. The first thing I found was a link to the Buck Nekkid website, which showcased covers of their bestselling DVDs and how to order them. The titles were real doozies too, like No G-Strings Attached, Meet the Fuckers, and American Dildo. When I tried to click off the site, 50 naked pop-ups invaded my screen. I yanked the cord from the wall.

It was time for me to go undercover because I needed some answers fast. It was already Friday and I'd promised Mike that I'd be back to work by Monday morning.

I found Melissa's card and called her. She asked if I could meet her at her loft in downtown Alpharetta at 3:30.

"I'll be there at 3:29," I said. I put her address in my GPS app on my cell. Then I kissed a picture of Denise and headed out the door.

When I got into the Cobalt, I pretended not to see the two white guys in black suits sitting in a black Buick across the street. This was a stakeout. I couldn't tell if they were local detectives, FBI, or hell, CIA. I just knew they were there for my ass.

After I hit the road, I spotted them three cars behind me like a bad TV show. Now this shit was getting crazy.

I wished I was in my Beemer. Push to start. Go from zero to 80 in seconds. Lose two goofy motherfuckers. In a little Chevy, it would be more of a challenge. I got my chance at a traffic light.

Most law enforcement agents rely on predictability. So I let them think I was predictable. I was driving northbound on Sugarloaf when I saw a yellow light and slammed on the brakes. One mile later, yellow light, boom, the brakes. Another mile, yellow light, and I punched it. The Cobalt's engine strained like a big burly baritone belting out Minnie Riperton. Zero to 30 in five long seconds. What the hell? Buy American my ass. Lucky for me, a long carrier truck got the green light on the westbound road. I checked my rearview, and when I still saw Mayflower, I made a quick right on a side street and another quick right and pulled into a parking garage. Lost them motherfuckers like virginity in a whorehouse.

I hopped out the car and checked it for tracking devices. Nothing. Stupid asses probably didn't even think of it.

When the coast was clear, I got back in the ride. I took some back roads to I-285. Then I hit 400 North headed up to Alpharetta. Checked my rearview a few times but saw no signs of the Buick. My heart was beating fast and my adrenaline flowed like I had just drunk a case of Mountain Dew and then ran the 400-Yard Dash.

Melissa's place was off Atlanta Highway, a three-story brick building that used to be an office building. When I got out the car, all I could smell was burned rubber from the tires and Krispy Kreme donuts from the building across the street.

She greeted me at the door dressed in a tight, white T-shirt with black letters that read DIRECT THIS and a picture of a hand flipping the bird. Nice tits too. They weren't any double dees like my baby had, but I could tell it was more than enough to put your dick between 'em.

"Right on time," she said and smiled. When she shut the door behind me, I sneaked a peek at her

ass. She filled out a pair of True Religion jeans
pretty well for a snowbunny. A baseball cap
covering her curly red hair completed the ensemble.

"I told you I would be," I said.

Her crib was nice. The walls were painted a
light shade of blue. A soft and plush sectional filled
the living room. The bedroom was connected, like a
living room and dining room would be. The king-
size bed looked big and comfortable behind shear
curtains attached to high end posts. The breakfast
nook, complete with granite countertops and tall bar
stools with leather seats gave the place a modern
look.

"Have a seat," she said and motioned towards
the sectional. "Can I get you anything?"

Some fucking answers, I thought. "I'll take a
beer if you got one."

She walked to the kitchen and opened the
fridge. "Bud Light okay?"

"That'll work."

I noticed she had framed snapshots on the glass
end tables and on the mantle over the pretend
fireplace. Over the fireplace was a picture of her
and some old people I assumed were her parents.
Another picture showed her in a bikini standing on
the deck of a yacht. The last one made my heart
race. It was Melissa, some balding guy, and my
baby, Denise. The fact that she knew her personally
told me I was getting close.

She returned with two bottles and a glass. "Just checking out your photos," I said. She handed me one of the bottles and a glass. She twisted off the lid of the other one and took a big sip. "Who are the people in the photo?" I asked.

She seemed happy to share. "Well this one," she said and pointed, "is a picture of me and my parents. It was their 25th wedding anniversary. And this one in the bikini was a party from work. And the other one is just a picture of me and some co-workers."

"That's a big boat. Is that Lake Lanier?"

"Mmm hmm." She looked at her feet when she answered. I knew better not to press any further just yet. "Please, have a seat."

I made myself comfortable on the sectional. Took a swig. I never cared for light beer, kind of tastes like somebody took a perfectly good drink and diluted it with water. Melissa sat diagonally across from me.

"So Karen tells me you could be the next John Holmes or something. She couldn't stop praising your glory." I almost laughed when she held her hands to the sky when she said praising, like she was in church.

"Oh that," I said. I tried to think of a clever way to tell Melissa just how Karen found out about my skills but drew a blank.

She must have sensed my discomfort because she touched my thigh and said, "Hey, you don't have to be shy with me. When you've been in the industry long enough, nothing shocks you."

"Karen tells me you can help me get in the game." I took another swig of the piss water.

"Yeah," she said. "I can get you in front of Monte Hill. He's the star director for Buck Nekkid Productions." She used air quotes when she said star. I could tell by her face that she didn't like this Monte character.

"So how'd you end up in the porn game anyway?" I asked.

"That's a long story. Here's the condensed version. Film school. Student loans. Bad Economy. No jobs, unless you want to fetch coffee for some cocaine-snorting director in Hollyweird. So you take a job as a lightning director in adult films and make three times the money you would in mainstream America. Case closed."

At that moment, I felt conflicted. I was starting to like this chick. Sounded like she had a good head on her shoulders. But still, if she was friends with Denise, why wasn't this bitch at the funeral?

"Sounds like this Monte dude better watch his back or you might take his job."

After that remark, she let out a big Kool-Aid smile. I looked into her green eyes and saw her pupils get bigger.

"Well anyway," she said. "I know you're eager and all but the best I can do is get you on the set as a stunt dick."

"A stunt dick? What the hell is a stunt dick?" I asked.

She laughed, stood up and took off her baseball cap, revealing more of that fascinating long, curly, red hair. "Oh, you *are* new to all of this, aren't you? How cute." I leaned forward, eager to hear her answer. "You know how a stunt man fills in and does all the fighting and breaking through glass and jumping off tall buildings for the high-paid actors in the movies?"

I nodded. "Yeah?"

"Okay. So a stunt dick fills in for the star when he can't get it up or if he can't come or if we need a big money shot and the star has no load."

While this information should have been a shock to me, it actually made me breathe a little easier. The last thing I needed was for my face to be all over some skin flick for some client or somebody like Ari to recognize me. If all I had to do was show my Johnson that would get me up close to some answers without revealing myself to the world. Hell, it even sounded cool. Ricky Stunt-Stunt Dick. Made you want to sing dah nah nah.

"Whatever I gotta do," I said.

"There's a catch though."

"Okay."

"Stunt dicks have to be on call, hard and ready at a moment's notice. Though, we usually shoot at night or on the weekends, sometimes we shoot in the middle of a workday. Is that going to be a problem?"

"I don't think so." I turned up the beer bottle.

"Great. Now if you would just take off your pants and show me what ya got, we'll be good to go."

I choked. Coughed. Beer shot out of my nose.

"Oh come on now Ricky. You're about to become a porn star. Surely you're not bashful."

There was that Kool-Aid smile again.

"Not at all."

I walked over to the fireplace since the lighting was better there. I pulled down my jeans, revealing a pair of red boxer briefs.

"Nice," she said. "Keep going."

I checked to make sure the curtains were drawn because the last thing I wanted to do was give a free peep show. When I took off my drawers, I could see the disappointment in her eyes. I wasn't hard.

"Oh. That could be a problem. What's wrong? You don't like me?" she asked. She walked towards me.

"No, it's not that. It's just that..."

She wrapped a cold hand around my dick and it rose like the sun. Her eyes grew wider than her smile when she saw it in all of its glory.

"Oh my," she said. "Oh my, oh my, oh my." She sounded like a broken record. The power of the penis has that effect on women.

"Normally I don't do this," she said.

Uh oh. Here it comes.

"But do you think I could, um, sample that?"

What the hell am I, a piece of meat?

I didn't just get off the boat. So when Melissa took off her T-shirt and bra like somebody pushed the fast forward button, I said, "Hell yeah you can."

She got down on her knees in front of me and started working me in her mouth like an ice cold Fudgsicle on a hot summer day.

I reached back and braced myself on the mantle with my right hand. Grabbed her head and guided it with my left. I ain't gonna lie. She knew her way around a dick. Guess it shouldn't have been a surprise, considering the hundreds of movies she must have helped film.

I came to the realization that I was going to have to fuck my way to the top to get to the bottom of it all. I don't know why I thought this chick was different. It didn't take long for Melissa to get completely naked.

She strolled over to her king size bed, lay on her back, and opened her legs. The drapes matched the curtains and the high beams. That was some sexy shit.

Her pussy was shaved, except for a strip, like a Mohawk. The shit looked good enough to eat so I put my tongue to work. I pitied that fool 'cause it was about to get beat up. When I looked up, her face was as red as her hair and her nipples stood erect like pencil erasers.

She came at the speed of light. Squirted like a mustard bottle. And I swear that elixir had my facial hair looking like Barry White when I came up for air.

She was a quiet one. Reached into the nightstand and pulled out a Magnum.

"Can I put it on you?" she asked.

No, I'm about to put it on you, I thought.

"Mmm hmm," I said. "But first let me get a taste of them sexy ass titties."

I honked one of them first. Palmed it like a baseball. Then I put the other one in my mouth.

Grabbed her ass with the other hand. She laid her head all the way back. Closed her eyes. Wet her lips. Used her free hand to play with my Willie. That shit was hot and I was ready to do some deep sea diving.

She sat up against the headboard, ripped open the package, and threw the wrapper on the floor.

I took off my shirt.

I kneeled in front of her on the bed and watched her roll it on me.

"Action," she said.

I gave her a little bit of the dick at a time. Played with her to see how she handled it. Sucked a breast in between strokes. She seemed to take it like a pro, so I went all in.

You would have thought somebody yelled, "Surprise," by the look on her face. "Holy shit," she yelled and reached for both bed posts. Grabbed them tight like a tornado was coming.

I pushed myself up above her like I was working out. Let her see the result of years of bench pressing. Then I thunder-pumped. Hard. Fast. Up. Down. Circles. Working my pelvis like my name was Elvis. I clenched my teeth and tried my damndest to reach her stomach.

After thirty minutes of this, I was ready to explode. Just as I was about to, her near silence was broken and she made a sound like a Holy War was about to begin. I could feel her pussy clenching my rod, and I couldn't help but come with her. Jihad motherfucker. I grunted loud, flopped on top of her, and our sweat became one.

As I got dressed in preparation of leaving she said, "You know. I have a good mind of keeping you to myself and not sharing you with the world." I looked at her, said nothing. "But I know that would be selfish. You have a gift, Sir Ricky. It would be a travesty *not* to share it."

"Is that a fact?" I asked.

"You'd better believe it."

I put on my shirt. Did the buttons.

"Oh. There's just a few more things," she said.

"Like what?"

"Well first, I would refrain from any recreational sex. You'll do well if you save it for the screen."

Now she tells me.

"Oh, and you should also get tested for STDs. Monte won't let you anywhere near the set without that piece of paper from a doctor. They do 'em in 48 hours over at Grady Memorial. You'll have to get tested weekly."

"Is that it?"

"Just a couple more things," she said. "I'll need your cell number in case we have a stunt dick emergency." I must have looked concerned because she said, "Don't worry. Most of our male actors are white anyway. We only have a few local black stars, and it's rare that they ever even need a stunt."

"Got it." I put on my shoes and searched for my keys.

"And can you be at the studio this Saturday at one? We're shooting a new film *Everybody Loves Bangin'*. We might be able to use you. I can introduce you to Monte. If he likes you, you're golden."

"I can do that."

"Great. It pays five grand."

"Five grand?" Five thousand dollars to have sex with beautiful women. Twenty movies would earn me one hundred grand. My face must have looked shocked.

"I know. It's kind of low. Don't worry, though. Once you're starring in movies that figure doubles."

Melissa eased off the bed, wiggled into her panties, and threw on a gray T-shirt. She had said the magic words I was waiting to hear: introduce you to Monte.

She walked me to the door, and I could tell she wanted to shove her tongue down my throat. Instead, she hugged me and gave me a peck on the cheek.

"Thanks for everything," I said and opened the door.

"No, thank *you* Ricky."

I smiled, trotted down the six flights of stairs, and made my way to the Matchbox I'd driven there.

I was getting close but the weekend was almost over and my two weeks off were nearly up. I would need to be patient and wait until next Saturday before I could start seeking my sweet revenge. In the meantime, I needed to focus on my real job.

Chapter 7

It didn't take long for Monday morning to come. And I was looking forward to a bit of normalcy in my life again.

Throughout the weekend, I camped out in the condo doing as much research I could about Buck Nekkid Productions, Melissa Summers, and Monte Hill. Saw a few articles about a guy named Stacy Prince and how he'd started the business.

My gut told me Monte was my guy. More digging revealed he was once a promising music video director in L.A., and he had directed a few Hip Hop videos. I guess it wasn't that big of a leap from video hoes to hoes with no clothes. IMDB showed some of his credits from when he was younger: production assistant on Dawson's Creek, 7th Heaven, and Undeclared. Then his credits disappeared like he had just fallen off the planet.

I used a people search website to find his address in Roswell. Then I used Google Earth to checkout satellite images of it. It was huge and even had a big swimming pool. Gotta love modern technology.

When I walked to my BMW Monday morning, I noticed there was no sign of the men in black. Just to be safe, I checked it for tracking devices but found nothing.

It felt good to be cruising in luxury and style again. The black leather interior seemed to welcome me back with its temperature control and my custom-made massage options. The only thing missing was Denise's smile staring back at me from the passenger's seat. I pushed the ignition button and headed to work.

White Mike greeted me at the door wearing a pink golf shirt and dark brown slacks. "Is everything all right?" he asked. He was biting his nails.

"Um, yeah. What's going on Mike?"

He looked around to see who was listening and said, "We need to talk, in private. Let's go to my office." He started walking there before I could even reply.

I hoped he and Ari hadn't blown the Moblicity deal. It was a big deal worth a lot of money, and I had put months of work into it.

When we got to his office, he shut the door and didn't bother to sit down.

"Friday, two FBI agents came around asking questions about you," he said.

I had a feeling they were Feds. What they wanted with me, I had no idea.

"What kind of questions?"

Mike paced the room. "All kinds of questions about how long I've known you. Is he a person you consider trustworthy? What do you know about his personal life? That kind of stuff."

This must have something to do with Denise's death, I thought. But how? What the heck did any of this have to do with a federal crime? Maybe it was nothing. Maybe they were just pissed off because I'd lost them when they tried to tail me.

"No worries Mike. I have no idea what they wanted but I assure you, I haven't committed any crimes, especially federal ones. Hell, I spent four years *fighting* federal crime in the Air Force. It wouldn't make any sense for me to do a 180 now. I got my own business, a nice condo, and a sweet ass ride. Life is good. So relax," I said and put my hands on his shoulders. "Everything is fine."

"I believe you, buddy, but I have to tell you, they got me to thinking. You *are* pretty hush-hush about your personal life."

"It's not because I'm smuggling cocaine in my ass cheeks from Mexico or running arms to the Taliban. I just don't like people all up in my business. Been that way since I don't know when. Work is work and home is home. And never the two shall meet."

"I hear ya man. But you'd better tell that to Ari. They asked him the same questions, and he is having some serious concerns."

"Don't worry. I'll deal with Ari. So how did the big meeting go?"

"Easy peasy. Had them eating out of the palms of our hands thanks to your presentation. Deal closed. First check in the bank."

"Now that's what I'm talkin' bout Willis." I high-fived him.

"Again man, sorry for your loss. If you ever need to talk, about anything, you know where to find me."

"It's a deal."

Chapter 8

The workweek flew by, not that it didn't have its share of disturbances. First I had to deal with my other partner, Ari.

"I'm sorry for your loss," he said. His eyes peered over his Sarah Palin-like glasses. Ari was a no-nonsense kind of guy. 50-year old Jewish guy from a long line of CPAs in the family, including both his parents, his grandfather, and two of his brothers. He stood about five nine, had an olive-like complexion, jet black hair cut short, and kind of a runner's body. Though not that big on fashion, he loved his Izod shirts and his slacks. Today he wore a light blue shirt and dark blue slacks.

"Thanks," I said while bracing myself for his bullshit.

"So who was it that passed away again?"

Nosey bastard.

"Let's just say, someone I loved and leave it at that."

"And I'm sure Mike told you about the federal agents."

"Sure did. And I'll tell you the same thing I told him. Nothing to worry about. I'm not doing anything illegal." I interlocked my hands and placed them on my desk.

"Fine, fine," he said and crossed his legs. "So about the financials..."

Finally, I thought. Back to business. Ari had a way of getting on my nerves when we weren't talking about the job.

"Yes?"

"The Moblicity deal put us right on track. Revenue is up. And now we should be able to leverage that deal to bring in the big fish." Ari smiled as he always did when it came to earning a profit.

"Panacea?"

"Bingo!"

"Fuck yeah," I said. "Get ready world. Here I come."

Ari gave me that look he always gave me when I cussed. But fuck that shit. I started the business and spoke the way I wanted to. As long as I didn't do it in front of clients, it wasn't a big deal to me.

"Um yeah. First meeting is next Tuesday. Gotta warn you though Ricky. These guys are strictly by the book. Ever since that anti-trust deal, I hear working with them is like dealing with the government."

"Don't worry, Ari. I'll run point on this one, and I'll be sure to win 'em over with my magnetism. You let me worry about the by-the-book stuff."

"Very well. They're flying in two marketing managers and a financial director, Jim Savitz. If all goes well, we fly out to Seattle for the second meeting."

"Well in that case, let me get started on this right now," I said, giving him his cue to leave.

He stood and smoothed out his slacks. "Just remember. This is the one we've been waiting for. We're talking millions."

"I'm on it, Ari."

Chapter 9

Before I knew it, Wednesday had rolled around. I was finally getting back into the groove of things, perfecting my pitch to Panacea, coaching my managers on overcoming objections on the phone, and even kidding around with Mike every now and then. Then I looked at my cell and thought of Denise and how much I missed her sexy texts, her beautiful smile, and the way we used to make love.

It all came back to me. I balled up my fists, clenched my teeth, and fought the urge to throw my iPhone out the window. Revenge could not come soon enough.

Just then, I remembered Melissa's words about needing to get tested. If it was a 48-hour turnaround, I would need to scoot down to the hospital today so that I could hand the papers to whoever needed them at Buck Nekkid Productions. I made it there an hour after work.

I could never stand hospitals. Needles. Disease. Blood and death. All that shit was a little too morbid for my ass.

I was greeted at the lab by a nurse's assistant. Ugly chick who made you consider giving up fucking all together. She was a dark sista with a ten-dollar weave and teeth like Mike Tyson's sparring partner. Throw-up green scrubs hung off her body. She wore a nametag that read Beatrice.

"May I help you?"

"Yes. I'm here to get tested for STDs." I searched her face for any signs of judgment. There were none.

"Do you have any symptoms?"

"Nope. It's just a precautionary thing."

She grabbed one of the many clipboards from a big pile of them and said in a dull tone, "I'll need you to complete this paperwork. There's a questionnaire regarding your medical history you need to complete front and back." She lifted a page. "Then there's a privacy statement I need you to sign and date."

She had her routine down pat. Sounded robotic with it. When she finished her speech, she smiled. With a face like that, I guess you have to be nice if you ever want to see a dick. Damn if she was ever gonna see mine, though.

When I finished the paperwork, Beatrice led me through the double doors behind her where a tall white guy greeted me.

"Hi. I'm Stan," he said and stuck out his hand. "I'm the charge nurse who'll be helping you with your testing today."

I shook his hand. "Ricky."

"Are there any particular symptoms you're experiencing?"

56

"Nope."

I know a man has got to eat but there are certain jobs he just shouldn't do. Flight attendant. Secretary. Stay-at-home dad. And yes, male nurse. I mean, how can you even get any ass? I could imagine telling a woman what I did for a living at a bar right before she laughed in my face.

But Stan was cool. He put my mind at ease, even when he got those needles and little tubes ready.

"So how 'bout those Braves?"

"They're looking pretty good. I think they have a shot this year."

He searched my arms for a vein and found a big fat one on my left arm.

"Me too. Pitching has been awesome. I'd love to see them beat the Yankees in the World Series." He stuck the needle in my arm and I felt a small pinch. "I grew up in Boston. And when you grow up in Boston, you learn to hate the Yankees."

"Oh yeah? I grew up in Detroit. We hated them too. Didn't stop them from kicking the Tigers' ass though."

I really didn't give a shit about the Braves, baseball, or Stan for that matter. I just wanted to get the shit over with so that I could get back to what I needed to do.

"Next," he said as he reached into a drawer in the exam room. "I'll need some urine." He handed me a packet with something that looked like a Handi Wipe and a clear plastic cup. "Just clean the tip of your penis with this first. Then pee into this cup.

I hopped off the exam table and did as he'd instructed.

When I returned, he had three long Q-tips laid out on a table. "And what are those for?" I asked as I handed him my urine.

"These are for your last three tests. We're going to test you for syphilis, gonorrhea, and chlamydia, the most common STDs." My eyes grew wide as I looked at the size of those things as they were almost as long as my dick.

"I need you to stand," he said as he picked up the first swab. "You'll feel a slight pinch." Then he jammed the thing up the tip of my cock.

Now I was ready to beat the shit out of Stan and call the fire department because it felt like my dick was on fire. I hadn't felt like that since I'd tried to wash it with soap and got soap inside of it.

"You're doing fine," he said as he put the Q-tip between two pieces of glass. I braced myself for the next one. He inserted it and I almost bit off my bottom lip. I tried to take my mind off of the pain by staring at the poster that showed how to recognize if you're having a stroke.

"We're almost done here," he said as he put in the last swab. I wanted to kick the wall by the time he was done. Then I thought about what Melissa said. I was going to have to go through this shit every week. Made me want to call the whole thing off right then and there.

"You said you're from Motown, huh? Great sports teams there, well, except for the Lions. The Red Wings are awesome though." He changed the subject in a flash. "We're done here. We'll have the results available in 48 hours." He reached into his blue scrubs' pants pocket and pulled out a business card. "Just call this number. Punch in your name and last four of your social security number. You'll get the results right over the phone."

"Actually, I need the results in writing and signed by a doctor for my, um, job. Is that doable?"

"Oh, sure. It's just that most folks would rather not come back here if they didn't have to. You know, in case the results are not what they hoped for."

"Oh, I'm not worried about the results."

"Cool. Well just come by the lab on Friday before eight or on Saturday morning. We're here at eight AM."

"Thanks Stan." I shook his hand and was back in my ride in no time.

On the ride home, a smidgen of doubt entered my mind. What if? For most of my life, I lived by the No-Glove, No-Love motto. But as I played back the highlight reels in my mind, I couldn't help but think about the few occasions of broken condoms and the fact that nobody knew for sure if you could get HIV just from oral sex. And then there was Denise. The only woman I ever really loved enough to go bareback with just happened to be a former adult film actress.

I wasn't pacing a hole in the floor or doing a LeBron James on my fingernails but the slip-ups in my past had me asking myself: What if I'm positive?

Come Friday morning, the buzz on my cell beat the alarm clock by about 30 minutes. It was a text.

Looking forward to seeing u in action tomorrow. Be sure to be there at 1:00 sharp. Don't forget your test results.-Melissa.

Bitch must be on the Espresso diet. Who the hell texts at o' dark thirty?

I replied: *I'll be there.*

Everybody Loves Bangin'. Thinking about the title alone made me say "ha" over my morning coffee and oatmeal.

I had a good day at work that Friday. Traffic didn't make me want to kill myself. Ari wasn't all up in my shit. And I had time to focus on my big

Panacea presentation up until the end-of-the-day staff meeting.

After work, I zipped over to Grady Memorial. Ugly Face was working the front desk again.

"Long time, no see," she said.

Not long enough, I thought while my balls tried to crawl up into my stomach. I smiled.

"Yes. I'm here to pick up my test results."

"Oh you didn't have to drive all the way down here. You could have called the Test Results line."

"I know," I said. "But I needed the results in writing for work."

"No problem. I can help you with that. I just need a photo ID."

I reached into my wallet and pulled out my Georgia driver's license. As I handed it to her, I said out of habit, "Not my best photo."

She laughed a little longer than she should have. I think she was trying to be flirty. I hoped she didn't think she had a chance with me.

She click-clacked on her keyboard, clicked the mouse a few times and said, "Here we go." I could hear the printer on the side of her humming and kicking out the paper. My heart starting doing double time.

After she handed me the paper, I really didn't want to read it in front of her. But the suspense was killing me.

My eyes zoomed past words: Richard Stunt. Lawrenceville. AB Negative. 48 Hour Test Results. And there it was in black and white.

Chlamydia-Negative. Syphilis-Negative. Gonorrhea-Negative.

HIV Negative.

I smiled and looked up at Beatrice who must have been studying me the whole time.

"Everything OK?" she asked.

"Couldn't be better," I said. "You have a good night."

"You too," she said and played with her hair a bit. Yeah, she was into me. The feeling was not mutual.

When you think about it, I guess I lied to Beatrice when I'd said things couldn't be better. Things could have been a helluva lot better if I had already found the mickey fickey responsible for Denise's death. But now I knew that day was coming soon.

Chapter 10

I got up at 10:00 Saturday morning. Showered.
Threw on a pair of Levi's and a tight, black T-shirt.
Made my way down to the rental car place. I'd
already turned in the Cobalt but I didn't want to
drive my BWM down to the studio.

Unfortunately, there was some sci-fi festival in
town. Geeks dressed up like Darth Vader and shit.
All they had left were mini-vans. I ended up taking
a Honda Odyssey.

The van had room enough for nine people and a
dog. It made me think of the family I would never
have with Denise.

Bastard gonna pay.

I made it to Atlantic Station at 12:30. With the
30 minutes I had to spare, I sat in the big green van,
with the AC running, and reviewed what I knew so
far on Buck Nekkid Productions, Melissa Summers,
and Monte Hill. I didn't have much to go on, but
my gut was telling me Monte was prime suspect
number one.

As I made my way into the building, Horny Ho
Karen greeted me.

"Well, well. Look who it is?" she said before
pulling on her right earring. She was standing and
wearing a bright, yellow sundress that revealed
enough cleavage to leave no room for imagination.

"Hey Karen. Been hangin' any coats lately?"

"Not in this hot weather," she said. Then the closet joke registered and she said, "Oh. Very funny Mr. Ricky."

"I'm just playin' with you. "

"I take it you're here for the shoot?"

"Yup. I was told to be here at one o'clock."

"In that case, follow me," she said and then grabbed a set of keys.

I followed her around the corner keeping in mind what happened the last time I did. As luck would have it, there was no closet, just elevator doors. She used a key to unlock the elevator but not before she palmed my ass like she was checking for fresh produce.

"Whoa. Didn't you get enough the last time?" I hopped onto the elevator and turned to face her as she stood in the lobby.

"I don't think I could ever get enough of you baby." I smiled as the elevator doors started to make her disappear. "Studio's on the top floor."

When the elevator doors opened, my perception of the industry changed forever. For many men, watching adult films is a thrill in itself. Getting paid to screw in one is like a fantasy come true. The first thing I noticed was the smell, and that's when the fantasy started to die.

There were three distinct smells fighting for superiority in the studio. The first was open ass.

Booty. Three-Day Old Farts. Whatever you want to call it, it was nasty. My cheeks puffed out but I didn't puke. The next smell was cum. Ejaculate. Semen. It reminded me of the times when I was a teenager and my mother would walk into my bedroom and know right away I had been stroking the one-eyed snake. A couple of sniffs and my secret was out. The last scent was Febreze. And though it fought a worthy battle, old cum and open booty kicked its ass.

The studio windows were all darkened out but there were lights everywhere. Track lights. White lights on the end of long lamps. Red lights, strobe lights, and even a traffic light.

Then there were the props. A king-sized bed, a living room set with a sectional, and even something that looked like a kitchen. Before then I had never seen a live movie set. As I tried to soak it all in, minus the funk, Melissa greeted me at the elevator doors.

"Ricky Stunt. So nice to see you again." She gave me a hug.

"Hey Melissa. Good to see you too." I hugged her back.

"So this is it! Welcome to Buck Nekkid. I'll show you to the dressing room so that you can get changed and meet the crew."

Changed? I thought. *Changed into what?* But then I remembered where I was and why I was there. *Changed into nothing.*

The dressing rooms were located just left and beyond the set, one for the women and the other for the men. Outside of them, I could hear the makings of several conversations going on. Laughter and high-pitched enthusiasm came from the women's dressing room. Deep voices came from the other.

I walked into the men's dressing room and all the chatter stopped in an instant. From the jump, they were sizing me up. There were four of them, two black guys, a white guy, and a brownish looking guy who could either be Hispanic of Middle Eastern from what I could tell. One of the brothers, who sat on a table with his feet in a chair, jumped up to greet me.

"You must be the fresh meat I hear was coming," he said. He was tall, about my height. Dark brown like a Hershey's bar. He wore his hair short and one length with a razor-sharp line up. His pants appeared to be a Velcro-like material, like the kind you tear away. His shirt was a red, Hawks jersey. With an upper body like a prizefighter, you could tell he got to the gym. "The name is Magnum Cum Loudly," he said.

I wanted to laugh in his face. Magnum Cum Loudly? What kind of a name was that? I thought only bitches bragged about cumming loudly.

"Ricky. Ricky Stunt."

Magnum looked as if a light bulb was over his head. "Oh yeah, right. Melissa told us about you. You're the new stunt dick and…" Magnum laughed out loud for a good 30 seconds. "Wait. Hold up. You mean to tell me your name is Ricky Stunt?"

"Yeah?"

"Is that short for Richard?"

"Right."

"And you're the stunt dick?"

"Okay, and?"

"Don't ya'll get it? We got us a stunt dick named Dick Stunt." Magnum laughed out loud again and this time the others joined in. "Sorry, man. That's just some funny shit," he said.

The white guy approached me next. "Pay no attention to Magnum. He likes to razz all the new talent. Just playing into his insecurities is all," he said with a straight-up Southern dialect. "They call me Jack Hammer," he said. Jack extended his hand.

"Whatchu trying to say Jack?" Magnum said.

"I ain't *tryin'* to say nothin'. I done said it."

"Ricky. Nice to meet you." I shook his hand. Jack appeared to be the oldest and the shortest of the bunch. I guessed he was about five six. Kind of reminded me of Larry the Cable Guy but without the gut. He wore a salt and pepper goatee and his hair looked like something from a Supercuts commercial or a congressional ad. Jack was in shape too but not gym shape. More like stay-at-home doing pushups and sit-ups shape. "Cmon over and meet the rest of the crew." He walked me over to the other two.

"This here is Phoenix," he said of the other black guy. Phoenix looked like he belonged in Hootie and the Blowfish or something. He stood about six four or six five. Wore his hair in a tan and black S-curl fro. He wore jeans and striped orange and blue suspenders over his bare chest. He looked too skinny to be in the game but then again, it takes all kinds.

"What's up, brother?" he said. Nodded his head when he said it but did not reach out his hand. "I'd reach out to shake your hand but I don't like to touch other dudes."

"No prob," I said. Truth was, I felt the same way.

"Yeah," the Hispanic-looking, Middle-Eastern-looking guy said with a slight Spanish accent. "He had one of those special uncles that made him that way." Everyone laughed except for me and Phoenix. "They call me Seven Point O," he said and then grabbed his Dockers at the crotch. "Cause that's what I'm packin'."

"More like O Point Seven," said Phoenix. The room filled with laughter again, and even I chuckled a bit at that one.

"Oh you got jokes huh?" said Seven Point O. "Do we need to pull out the ruler and shut you up once and for all?"

"That's where you wrong you no-speaky-English mofo. Ya'll gone need a yard stick to measure my shit."

"Yeah right," he said over the oohs, aahs, and laughing.

"So whatchu packin' Ricky?" Magnum asked causing the laughter to subside.

"I don't know. I don't sit around measuring my shit. I let the ladies worry about how big it is, and I ain't never had a complaint," I said. Then I looked him straight in the eyes and said, "If you ask me, that's a faggotity-ass question anyway."

Magnum's eyes narrowed and his fists became weapons. He kicked over a chair and leaped at me. "Why you disrespectful motherfuckah," he said as threw a punch at my left cheek. I moved just in time to hear the punch whoosh in the air next to me. "You ain't nothin' but a stunt dick and you already startin' some shit!"

Phoenix and Jack Hammer moved like lightning. Phoenix locked Magnum's arms behind his back. "Whoa, whoa, whoa. Hold it brother!" he said. Jack stood between me and Magnum and stretched out his palms to our chests to keep us away from each other. Magnum continued.

"You better watch who you calling faggot, nigga. That kind of shit will have your ass dead and washing up on the shores of Lake Lanier."

Magnum may as well have said. "I killed Denise." Without haste, I pushed Jack out of my way and punched Magnum in his goddamn face. Then Seven Point O jumped up and grabbed my arms to restrain me. "Man," I said. "You don't know who you fuckin' with but you 'bout to find out."

Magnum pushed his tongue into his cheek and made it puff out. After he spit blood, he checked himself in the vanity. He grabbed a hand towel and pressed on the bleeding spot. "That was a sucker punch. You lucky Phoenix was holding me back."

Yeah but who's gonna hold me back from you when I get another chance, I thought. As far as I was concerned, Magnum had just become prime suspect number two.

Just then, Melissa knocked on the dressing room door and entered before there was a reply. "Five minutes til showtime guys," she said. Then her eyes grew wide at the sight of the room's disarray, Magnum's tending to his face, and me looking like I was mad at the world. "What's going on here?" she asked.

The room was silent before Seven Point O replied, "Nothing to worry about Melissa. Just a little new guy hazing. Everything is fine."

"New guy hazing huh? You guys better watch yourselves. You know how Monte gets about continuity and stuff, especially when it comes to his superstar."

Magnum caught my eye from the reflection in his vanity and smiled. "You hear that stunt dick. *I'm* the superstar around these parts."

"Not for long," I said.

"Come on Ricky. I think there's a little too much testosterone in here. I need you to come with me so that I can introduce you to Monte." She put her arm around mine, and we left the room together.

As we walked towards the set, she asked, "What happened in *there*?"

"Like dude said. Just a little hazing. You know. Nobody likes the new guy."

"Well if I were you, I'd tone it down a bit. Monte is a no bullshit kind of guy. Any sign of a problem, and you're out here like that," she said and snapped her fingers.

"My bad. Your boy Magnum Cum Lousy just rubbed me the wrong way that's all."

"Yeah. He has that effect on people, especially those he sees as a threat. You think that's something, just wait 'til he finds out about your special gift."

"You mean my package?"

"Package. Gift. All the same thing."

Finally we arrived to the set and there sat the man who could only be Monte Hill. I scoped him from toe to head. He wore expensive looking Bruno Magli shoes, a pair of dark dress slacks, a white polo with blue strips, and a beret that did not fully cover his balding head. Though he looked in our direction, he didn't even acknowledge me.

"Melissa, what the hell is going on? We're already fifteen minutes late. We were supposed to start shooting at one."

"Sorry Monte. The girls were having a bit of a wardrobe malfunction and Diamond was trying to remember her lines."

"Jeesh. What do they think this is? Network TV?"

Melissa tried to break the tension with a little laugh but Monte didn't crack a smile. Monte took off his hat and smoothed over his shiny head before putting it back on.

"I know. It shouldn't be more than five minutes or so."

"Whatever. Let's just put a move on."

"Oh, Monte. This is the guy I told you about. Ricky Stunt."

I played the fan role. "Nice to meet you Mr. Hill. I'm a big fan of your work." I extended my hand. He didn't take it.

"Oh you like the skin flicks, huh? What's your favorite, Slutty Housewives Number Five, or something more modern like Perry Hotter?"

Perry Hotter. I'd seen a clip of the flick online. Dude dressed like a wizard from the waist up and naked from the waist down. He was running around thrusting his pelvis and shouting, "Ree-dick-you-lous!"

"Actually, I was referring to some of your earlier work. I really liked that L.L. Cool J. video you directed. The cinematography is nice!"

You could tell Monte was impressed, although he wouldn't give me the satisfaction. Instead he said, "Well let me tell you. If you're thinking about using this as a stepping stone to music or something, you can forget about it. Porn is a one-way ticket. Like I tell all my actors, if you can make it here, you can't make it anywhere."

"That's not…"

"Um, that's not something you need to worry about Monte," Melissa said interrupting me.

"Good. So what are you packing, uh..?" he asked and looked at Melissa.

"Ricky," she finished.

"Yeah. Ricky."

"We haven't measured him yet, but trust me, from what I saw, he's an eight. Easily an eight."

"An eight huh? This I gotta see. Okay, er, Ricky. Show me whatcha got?"

This was the second dude interested in seeing my junk. Maybe it was just how they rolled in the industry, but that shit felt so wrong.

"But I'm not even hard," I said.

"Hard, smard. If it's big limp, I know it's big hard. Come on. Pull it out. Don't be bashful."

I looked at Melissa who gave me a well-go-ahead kind of look. "Why the heck not?" I said. I dropped my Levi's and my drawers to the floor around my ankles. Monte's eyes grew wide as did Melissa's smile.

"Told ya," she said.

Chapter 11

Ten minutes later, the rest of the Atlanta crew was assembled on the set, and I was standing on the sidelines with Melissa while she did her thing. There were set guys everywhere with lights, little cameras, holding that big mic. Some guys seemed to be just standing around getting a free show.

There was no time for introductions to the actresses as things were already running a bit late. But by the time Monte yelled, Action," I pretty much knew who everyone was.

First, there was Diamond, a hot little firecracker that stood about five feet even. She was midnight black and beautiful, like an African princess. Her hair was straight, down to her shoulders and as far as I could tell, it was not a weave. She looked like she knew her way around a StairMaster and maybe an elliptical by the look of her lower body. Diamond had the kind of ass that only a sista could have and just enough boobage to put your hands around. She wore a halter top and a short mini skirt. She also wore a diamond belly button ring.

Then there was Amber, the blonde goddess. My guess was that she was about five feet eight. Beautiful. Looked like she should have been on America's Next Top Model instead of shooting this kind of stuff. She wore a bikini top, jeans, and shoes with three-inch heels. Though her tan looked fake, she sure wasn't faking when she caught a glimpse of me. Licked her lips like my shirt said KFC. Now I had wood despite the cum/booty/Febreze odor.

There was an Asian chick, too. Couldn't tell if she was Chinese, Korean, or Vietnamese but she was cute in her own sort of way. She was skinny and had a flat chest. Her backside looked like her legs were attached to one long back. Her hair was long and straight and her face was nice. They called her Princess.

Finally, there was the brunette who went by the name Sugar Tits McGee. And judging by the way those double-dees busted out of the tight, white T-shirt she wore with no bra, it was no wonder. Nothing but Nipple City up under there. Her face was a cross between Pamela Anderson and Katherine Hegel. Her super short shorts showed her assets very well. She had a winter-type body; the kind you want to come home to and snuggle up with after a day in below-freezing weather.

The bevy of tits and ass almost made me forget why I was there. But Sugar Tits reminded me of Denise and I almost blew my top. And now I already had two guys I was ready to kill.

"Pay close attention to Magnum," Melissa said. "He's a real pro." I wondered if she learned of his skills the same way she'd found out about mine.

"Oh don't worry. I'm watching him like a hawk." *That kind of shit will have your ass washing up on the shores of Lake Lanier.* I imagined my hands around his neck.

Magnum went at Princess hard. First from a missionary position. She yelled, "Oh fuck me," and other sounds but it all seemed fake to me. If she was wearing a watch, I think she would have peeked at it. He shouted, "Take this dick!" and glanced over at me. But from what I could tell, she could take it or leave it.

Meanwhile, Sugar Tits rode Jack Hammer on the floor and those sugar tits bounced up and down like super balls. Jack Hammer moved under her like the Bionic Man.

Seven Point O had Amber bent over the kitchen sink, holding her waist and plunging into her from behind. He grunted and she moaned. She let out a few "ahh yeahs."

Diamond had her legs wrapped around Phoenix's waste and he stroked from on top of her. "Fuck me daddy," she shouted. "Fuck me!" Her command made him go harder and faster.

By then, Monte had left the director's chair and was moving around between the four couples with a handheld camera. As he approached each of them, he barked out commands like a drill instruction. *Grab her hair. Switch to doggie style. Put it between her tits. No. No. No. Like this!* No wonder they were getting ten grand a picture. The psychological stress alone was worth it.

With Monte being distracted and Melissa seeming to trust me more, I figured it would be a good time to find out what she knew.

"So Melissa. Magnum said something to me about ending up dead at Lake Lanier. You have any idea what he was talking about?"

Melissa's face turned red and she kept her eyes on the set as she spoke to me. "That stupid asshole. He said what?"

"You heard me."

"It's nothing. There was an accident a few weeks ago and, shit! I can't believe he said something like that. Nothing Ricky. Nothing."

I pushed her for more. "Yeah. I saw something about that on the news. I knew it had something to do with an ex-porn star but I didn't know it was someone from here."

"Not here," she whispered. "Can we talk later?"

"I'm 'bout to come!" Phoenix shouted. I turned from Melissa to the set. Monte had yelled cut and Diamond got some new pearls to go with her diamond stud.

"What the hell Phoenix? Are you jacking it at home or something!"

"No," he said. He looked down at the floor and then around the room.

"You're done for today. Karen has your check downstairs."

"But I can go again Monte. Just give me 15 minutes."

"I don't have 15 minutes. We're already late as it is."

Phoenix stood up and made his way towards the dressing room watching his feet the entire time. By the time he made it there, Magnum let out a huge laugh.

"You are such a dick," Diamond said.

"What?" he replied. "I told him to start doing them kegels. Six months in the game and still acting like a rookie."

"All right everybody, back into positions," Monte instructed.

After a bit of grumbling, they all gathered themselves, climbed back on top of each other. Then Monte looked over at me. "Okay stunt dick. You're up."

I had a good mind to say, "Whatchu talkin' 'bout, Willis?" But Monte was a no-nonsense kind of guy. So instead of saying a word, I dropped my pants and my drawers in one motion. In a whirlwind, that big watermelon smile on Magnum's face disappeared.

Yeah bitch. This is what I'm working with.

The drill sergeant started up again. "All right Ricky. I know this is your first time at the rodeo, so

I'm going to lay it down real simple for you. All I need is ten more minutes of footage and a money shot. Do you think you can bust one off on cue?"

I wanted to bust a cap in his chrome dome real fast.

"Well. I'm used to pleasing the ladies first…"

"Don't worry. There'll be plenty of time to prove your bravado. But right now, I need you to give me ten minutes, get yours fast, pull out, and give me my money shot."

"I can do that," was what I said. But my mind was saying, *Welcome to the wonderful world of AIDS*. But I knew I had to put that way of thinking to the back of my mind. I just hoped the weekly STD testing was legit.

As I made my way to Diamond, I closed my eyes a few seconds and thought about Denise and how she used to turn me on by just smiling at me, let alone the good sex we had in bed, on the floor, in the BMW. I was a rock.

Diamond stuck out her hand. "Diamond," she said and smiled. "Nice to meet you."

"Nice to meet you too," I said and shook her hand. Then Monte yelled, "Action," and aimed the camera straight at my crotch.

I didn't have time to ease it in. You know, give her five, six, seven, eight. Who does she appreciate? Instead I went all in. And she yelled, "Holy shit!"

and her eyes looked like I was Jason and it was Friday the 13th. But I was killing her with the dick.

I grabbed her by her shoulders, bit my bottom lip, and tried to fuck her through the couch. I did it hard. I did it fast. Ten minutes of this and I could feel her clench, and then she said, "I can't believe this shit. I'm about to cuummmmm!"

And that's when I said, "Me too."

I pulled it out and watched my load shoot up to her tits and drip through the crevices of her belly.

"And cut," said Monte.

Everyone except for Monte and Magnum applauded. "Good job," Seven Point O yelled.

"Nice work," Sugar Tits added.

"Thanks," I said. Then I walked off the set to retrieve my clothes and finish the conversation with Melissa.

"Nice work," she said. "I could tell Monte was impressed."

I gave the room a once over. As the actors and Monte prepared to wrap things up shooting their final scenes, many of them smiled at me and gave me the thumbs up. But Magnum sulked because he feared I was about to take his spot. Little did he know that if I found out he had something to do with Denise's death, his spot was the last thing he had to worry about.

"There's a cast party tonight over at Fox Sports Bar. You should come. No pun intended."

"I'll think about it."

After the shoot, I tried speaking with Monte for a few minutes, but he was not having it.

"Nice work in there," he said as he looked at the camera equipment he'd gathered up. I could have easily grabbed one of the cords and wrapped it around his neck. But first, I just needed proof that he deserved it.

"Hey, thanks for the opportunity. I was a bit nervous at first."

"Yeah, who isn't? This ain't the Mickey Mouse Club we're shooting here."

"True. Plus when Magnum mentioned that woman dead at Lake Lanier that made me ask myself what I had gotten myself into."

Monte didn't take the bait. Instead he kept his silence and tried to finish putting cameras in cases. I pressed on.

"I heard about that woman on the news. Do you know anything about that?"

Monte dropped the equipment, turned to face me and made eye contact. I watched as his face scrunched up and his eyes narrowed.

"Now listen here and listen good," he said. He poked his finger in my chest. "If you want to end your career before it even begins then keep asking questions and putting your nose where it doesn't belong. Are we clear, stunt dick?"

It took everything in me not bash him in the face with my bare knuckles. A refusal to answer questions was as good as guilty in my book. I didn't want the bastard to know what I was up to, so I played the role. Put my hands up like somebody yelled, 'This is a stick up,' and said, "crystal."

He liked my reply. Lightened up and even smiled a bit. "Now why don't you go, get your check and celebrate a job well done. And remember, there's plenty more where that came from."

I didn't like the way he stonewalled me, but I figured there would always be the cast party. Maybe if he got a little liquored up, he'd spill his guts and then *I* would spill his guts all over the streets of Atlanta.

After I got my check, I went home. Jumped in the shower and scrubbed off all of Diamond's juices and Phoenix's sloppy seconds. I almost puked at the thought of it. I had done some freaky shit in the sheets, but I had never went up in a woman just after another dude finished.

As I prepared to get in the mini-van to head back to Atlantic Station, I spotted the Feds again. I wracked my brain trying to figure out what the hell they wanted with me. As I pulled away, I checked the rearview to see if they would tail me again. Luck was on my side because there was no way in hell I was going to lose them driving an Odyssey.

It was dark by the time I made it to the Fox
Sports Bar. Inside, the bar was jammed pack and
loud. Several large flat screens showed the Braves
game. Many of the customers drank beer, ate bar
food, and yelled at the TV screens. The hostess
greeted me at the door. She was a cute little thing.
Brown like a Reese's Cup and voluptuous like a
pin-up girl. She wore a white blouse, black skirt,
and black stockings.

"Hi. May I help you?" she asked and smiled.

"I'm here to meet some friends," I said.

Just then I heard a woman calling my name
over the cheers of the crowd.

"Rickeeee. Rickeeee. Over here!"

It was Melissa, waving her outstretched hand
from a booth in the corner.

"Never mind," I said to the hostess. "I see
them."

I walked past tables filled with pizza, hot
wings, burgers, and lots of alcohol. The food
smelled good and made my stomach grumble. As I
approached the booth, I started to see the faces from
earlier that day. Sugar Tits, Diamond, and Amber
took up one side of the booth. Magnum and Jack
Hammer sat on the other side.

Melissa stood up to greet me.

"Hi Ricky," she said. She hugged me, kissed
me on the cheek, and balanced a cocktail in her

hand. I hugged her back. "So glad you could make it."

"Hey Melissa," I said. The table was filled with pitchers of beer, empty shot glasses, and a half-eaten pizza. Everyone but Magnum smiled and greeted me with a mixture of hellos, welcomes, and what's ups. Magnum took a swig of beer and just mean-mugged me.

"So this is how they party at Buck Nekkid huh?"

"No. The party was at the studio earlier today. This is the after party," said Sugar Tits. The booth was packed so I grabbed a chair from another table and scooted it on the end of the booth.

"What do you want to drink?" Melissa asked.

"Jack."

"What?" said Jack Hammer.

"Not you Jack. I was just telling Melissa…" Before I could finish, the table busted out in laughter.

"I'm just pulling your chain," Jack Hammer said.

"Oh I get it. Razzing the new guy, huh?"

"I'll go find our waitress," Melissa yelled and made her way towards the bar leaving me with just the actors.

"Looks like ya'll been partying," I said as I looked at all the empty glasses. "Where is Phoenix and Monte?"

"Monte never comes to these kinds of things. He's a little uptight in case you didn't notice," Amber said.

"Yeah. And Phoenix had other plans," Jack Hammer added.

"Hmmph. Plans my ass. Embarrassed is more like it," Magnum replied.

"Would you just chill?" Diamond snapped. "Why you always on his shit?"

"Whatever," Magnum said. Then he took a few gulps of his beer. "So, stunt dick, what made you decide to get in the game?"

Ain't this a bitch? I thought. He should be fielding *my* questions.

I decided to humor him. "Well you know, I was always told I had a gift."

"You got that right," Diamond added. I chuckled.

"So I figured, it would be a shame not to share this gift with the world and make a little money too."

"From what I saw, I wouldn't mind sampling that gift of yours myself," Sugar Tits said.

"Well don't get your hopes up. Stunt dicks come and go," Magnum said. Everyone at the table laughed out loud.

"Damn right they do," Amber said. She held up her shot glass and Diamond clinked it with hers.

"Ya'll know what I meant," Magnum added. Then Melissa appeared with two shot glasses filled with Jack Daniels.

"What did I miss?" she asked as she handed me the glasses.

Just then, the place erupted with cheers. "Hell yeah," one man said. "Grand slam!" another added.

"Thanks for the drinks!" I yelled over the noise.

"No problem. You've got some catching up to do."

I took a shot of Jack. Nursed the other one. I looked around the booth and as far as I could tell, everyone was already buzzed or almost drunk. Now would be the perfect time to find out who knew what.

"It's a shame about that girl they found at Lake Lanier," I said and watched happy faces turn solemn.

"Yeah," Amber said. "Denise was *so* nice."

"Oh, you knew her?"

"We all knew her," Diamond added. "She was too good for this business. I still can't believe she's gone."

"Diamond, please. That bitch knew what she was getting into. She was a grown ass woman," Magnum added. I counted his comment as another reason to whoop his ass.

"What do you think happened to her?" I asked looking more at the women than the men.

"Probably at the wrong place at the wrong time," Sugar Tits said.

"You know what they say: snitches end up in stitches," Magnum said and then smirked. My blood boiled.

"Oh cool it, Magnum. You act like you were there or something. Heck, none of us were there. As far as we all know, it was an accident," Melissa said.

Did my ears deceive me? None of them were there? Why was I thinking this happened at some kind of cast party out on a yacht?

"Well I might not have been there but I hear things. We all hear things, don't we?" Nobody bothered to reply. Instead they stared at their drinks, the window, and the TV screen, anywhere but at each other.

"What kind of things?" I asked.

"Look here, stunt dick."

"The name is Ricky, Magnum Cum Lousy."

"Well whatever yo' name is, you sholl asking a lot of questions. Whatchu a cop or something?"

Suddenly all eyes were on me and they looked concerned. I had to put their minds at ease. "A cop? Negro you must be crazy. Did you not just see me boning the hell out of Diamond?" I looked to her and said, "No offense."

She replied, "None taken."

"Now I don't know about you but I ain't never heard of a cop going *that* deep undercover." The women laughed and Jack Hammer smiled.

"So what's with all the questions then?"

"I just want to make sure I ain't got myself into something I can't get out of."

"Hey, hey, hey," Melissa said. "In case you guys forgot, this is a party. Now let's drink up and have ourselves a good time." Melissa turned up a shot glass filled with a clear liquid. My guess was that it was Tequila.

"I'm with you on that, Melissa," added Jack Hammer. He raised his beer mug and said, "To Buck Nekkid!"

We all chimed in, "to Buck Nekkid!" But in mind I was thinking, *to hell with Buck Nekkid.*

Chapter 12

When I awakened that Sunday morning at home, I felt no closer to solving Denise's murder than I did from the jump. Now I had to go back to the drawing board. Magnum, Melissa, and the Everybody Love Bangin' cast weren't even in the area when Denise was killed. Something told me, the answer would come from Monte. But he wasn't saying a word. I'd have to find another way to make him talk.

In addition to this, I had my big Panacea presentation Tuesday morning. So for the rest of the day, I worked on my PowerPoint, did my research on their staff, and practiced my presentation in front of the mirror.

Denise's death kept gnawing at me, so I went online and did more research. Buck Nekkid Productions. Stacy Prince. Monte Hill. I woke up Monday morning with my face planted in the keyboard. Luckily, I had saved my presentation.

Monday flew by and before I knew it, it was Tuesday and showtime. I was in the main conference room with Mike, Ari, and the threesome from Panacea. I was on too. I even looked good in my dark brown, three-piece Armani suit.

"So what we've learned is that a combination of voice mail, e-mail, and direct mail makes a kind of swarming effect on the prospect. Once they hear the messaging from all sides, they become familiar with the campaign and decide to take a next step. And with a brand name like Panacea, it's a no brainer." The three of them were eating out of the palm of my hand. Even Ari seemed to be impressed.

Their finance guy chimed in. "Looks good to me but The Phone Room is relatively new in the marketplace. Why should Panacea go with you instead of another more established company?"

"I'll give you three reasons," I said. Then I felt my cell phone buzz. I pulled it from my belt and saw that it was an incoming text from Melissa.

9-1-1. Phoenix was a no show for a shoot. Need u on set in 30 min. Can u make it?

My palms moistened. Heart felt like it was tap-dancing. And my mouth became the Mojave. *This cannot be happening now,* I thought.

"Everything all right?" Ari asked.

"Um, sure, fine. Can I see you and Mike in the hallway for a minute?" I said and started walking towards the door before they replied. "Would you excuse me?" I asked the potential clients.

"What's going on Ricky?" Mike asked me. "You look like you've seen a ghost."

"Something has come up. I have to go."

"What do you mean something has come up?" Ari replied. "Do you know who is in there? It's goddamn Panacea!"

"I know and I'm sorry. Mike, can you take over? You crushed it with the Moblicity guys. I know you can do it here too."

"No, Ricky. I had more time to prepare for Moblicity. I don't have much intel on this one. We need you on this one buddy."

"All you have to do is follow the PowerPoint. I'll catch up with you later today and we can talk about next steps."

"Listen Ricky. I don't know what you're into but I can tell you this. If you blow this deal, it's going to be the end of this partnership," Ari said.

"Sorry fellas. It's an emergency." I looked at my iPhone and my partners' flabbergasted faces before jetting out the building and getting into my car.

I felt like Mario Andretti in my Beemer. I may as well have put the car on cruise control when I hit 80 because that was the lowest speed I hit on I-85. Thank goodness none of Atlanta's finest clocked me and pulled me over.

I flew up to Karen, and she ran with me to the elevator. Didn't even say a word. I guessed she was told of the emergency as well.

The first face I saw was Magnum's. He rolled his eyes like a little bitch. Then I saw Melissa. "You didn't have to get all dressed up," she said. I'd completely forgotten I was wearing my Sunday's best for the presentation.

"Oh, this. I had something else to attend…"

"Doesn't matter. Anyway, Phoenix is MIA. I tried calling him, paging him, nothing."

For the first time, I noticed the set was different. It looked like the inside of the oval office. At second glance, Magnum was wearing a suit.

"I know it's short notice but this just might be your big break."

"What do you mean?"

"What I mean is this is a feature role. There's even lines for you."

This was not what I wanted to hear. Though I wanted the opportunity to get to Monte again, I did not want my face plastered all over a freakin' porno. I imagined the look on my clients' faces when they popped in a flick at home only to discover my face. Not to mention if Mike and Ari found out.

"I thought this was a stunt role. I don't know if I'm ready for a feature. I'm no actor."

"Have you seen a porno lately? In case you didn't know it, all the acting is terrible. Nobody really gives a damn. You just show 'em that huge rod of yours and you'll be an instant star."

I was at a crossroad. If I said no, then my investigation would be over and I might never find out who killed Denise. But if I said yes, then it could very well end my real career. I thought about it a few seconds. Maybe if I could just get to Monte and ask him the right questions, I wouldn't have to go through with it.

"Where's Monte?" I asked her.

"Bathroom. Why?"

"No reason. Just wondering what he thought of me acting, that's all."

"Does that mean you're in?"

"Just let me get changed," I said and headed towards the dressing room.

"There's a few costumes in there. I'm sure you'll find one that fits you. If not, no worries. It won't be on for long. Oh, and there's a script too. Look for the lines for Agent Smith."

When I was out of Melissa's sight, I headed a few doors down to the men's room. Monte was washing his hands.

"Ricky," he said. His voice bounced off the walls. "Glad you could make it on such short notice. I don't know what the hell is going on with Phoenix."

"Well, when one door closes another one opens."

Monte turned off the spigot and reached for the paper towels. "Exactly," he said as he dried his hands.

"You don't think anything's wrong with Phoenix do you?"

"Doubt it. Probably just his ego bruised or just being his usual irresponsible self."

I walked to the urinal. Undid my zipper. "He didn't show up for the cast party either. I mean first everyone's talking about some ex-porn star drowning and now Phoenix is missing. I'm starting to think this is an occupational hazard."

"First of all," he said over the sound of my piss hitting water. "The papers got it wrong. She was no star. She was a good assistant though. Denise clearly belonged behind the cameras and not in front."

"Magnum said she was a snitch," I said as I shook off my peter.

"Magnum," he said. "He's like a chick. Trust me. As long as you keep your nose out of business that doesn't concern you, you'll make a lot of money here and have a lot of fun doing it. I gotta go get prepped. See ya out there."

Back in the dressing room, I sat in Phoenix's chair. There on the desk in front of me was the script for The Audacity of Hoes. The script was thin like a pamphlet. I flipped through it and looked for the lines for Agent Smith:

"You're about to feel this stimulus package."

"All hail to the commander in briefs."

"The only party I'm affiliated with is the one in your panties."

Clearly, I didn't need to be a trained thespian to deliver those cheesy ass lines. I looked at myself in the mirror and then switched into one of the costumes; a secret service-looking getup with pants tight enough to see the imprint of my cock in front.

Sugar Tits and the three Ms were on set.

"Nice fit," Melissa said. "Are you ready for your first feature?"

"Does a duck quack?" I asked.

"I can see it now," she said. Raised her hands in the air as if she was framing the words. "Magnum Cum Loudly, Sugar Tits McGee and, uh. Oh crap! I just realized, you haven't picked out a name."

"Oh. I thought his name was Stunt Dick," Magnum replied.

"And I thought your name was Shut the Fuck Up," I told Magnum.

"You want a piece of me, stunt dick?" he said and inched towards me.

"Okay, okay fellas. Let's save the action for the screen," Melissa said while jumping in between us. "Now where was I? A name for you. Hmm. Ricky Stunt-the eight inch wonder. No. Rick Stunt. Big Dick Stunt. No. I guess we don't *have* to use your real name."

"How 'bout Dick Stunner?" I asked. "Stunning the ladies with eight inches of pure pleasure."

"I like that one," Sugar Tits chimed in.

"Yeah. Me too. It has a nice ring to it minus the subtitle," Melissa contributed.

"Sure beats Magnum Cum Lousy," I said.

"It's Loudly motherfucker. Loud-ly."

"The shit is gay no matter how you say it. Come Loudly." I shook my head.

Monte commanded, "OK. Places everyone."

I got near the set and waited for my cue. Meanwhile, Magnum and Diamond delivered their corny lines and commenced to fucking. The thing about Magnum was that his acting wasn't that bad. Sounded just as good as anything I'd seen on a sitcom. A real sitcom, not the Playboy Channel. If young buck hadn't discovered the porn world, he probably could have made it in Hollywood. Of course, I would never have told his faggot ass that.

When it was my turn to hit the set, I realized that everything had changed. No longer would I have an anonymous dick exploding on a screen near you. Now my face was going to be immortalized for strangers, friends, and the whole wide world to see.

Sugar Tits was naked and waiting for me. Not only was I about to enter Sugar Tits, I was about to enter some shit I had never expected to get into, my face on camera.

With all the set guys and actors looking on it felt like a million eyes were all on me. The room came to a hush. I readied myself to deliver my lines.

"I'm about to show you a stimulus package," I said.

"From what I'm seeing from here," Sugar Tits said, "you already have my vote."

Why a secret service agent even had a stimulus package, I had no idea. But this wasn't for prime time. Hell, most people fast-forwarded to the sex scenes when they bought this stuff anyway.

Sugar Tits walked to a large oak desk. Her body was fine. She had thighs that looked like they could crack a walnut. Breasts like melons. And real washboard abs.

I stood in front of her. She looked at my erection and smiled. I caressed her breasts. Brought my head down to one of them. Kissed and sucked. The other hand played with the other breast.

She flipped her hair and held her head back as if she was staring at the ceiling. Her hands rubbed my back. Grabbed my ass.

"Enough of the foreplay," Monte barked. "Let's earn our paychecks people."

Sugar opened her legs wide. Her pussy was shaved. Not a hair to be seen. I used my hand to guide my dick into her. She wrapped her legs around my waist.

I tried to ignore the fact that all those people were in the room and focused on her banging body.

I thrust slow-motion style. Then harder. She used her legs to bring me in even more. The camera was aimed at our crotches. About seven minutes of this went on before Monte said, "OK. Let's see you ride him Sugar."

She stood. Made room for me to sprawl out on the desk. I lied on my back. Everyone was looking at my dick as it pointed to the ceiling. She straddled me with her face facing away from me. I heard the desk creak and hoped we didn't come crashing down to the floor.

Her pussy wasn't the tightest I'd ever had but the juices flowed like a fountain.

Monte aimed the camera at her face, her tits, and her pussy riding my cock. Like clockwork, seven minutes passed and Monte asked us to switch.

"I need a money shot in this next sequence. Can you do that for me Ricky?"

I smiled at Sugar and answered, "I don't think that will be a problem."

She got down on her hands and knees on the floor. The rug under her had the presidential seal on it. I got down on the floor behind her. The front of my thighs touched the back of hers. She reached back and rubbed my dick.

I grabbed her waist and she guided me into her wetland. I pumped in and out. She said "Fuck me baby." My pelvis picked up the pace like a piece of machinery.

"Oh yeah," she said. "Just like that." Seven minutes of this had my balls screaming for a release.

"All right Ricky," Monte said and looked at his watch. "It's time for my…"

I pulled out my dick and sprayed my juice all over her ass and back. Let out a loud caveman grunt.

"…money shot. Damn! Right on time."

After the spasms, I fought off the urge to give her a hug and to thank her for being patient with a rookie. But that would have made me look soft. So I smacked her ass and said, "Good job."

"Same to you. You're a regular pro."

The set people applauded. Gave me at-a-boys and pats on the back.

When it was over, I picked up my check for ten grand at the front desk and walked Melissa to her ride. My company would have had to make 2500 hours' worth of cold calls for this kind of money.

"You were amazing in there Ricky. Did you see the look on Sugar Tits's face when you gave her the full eight?"

"You mean that look of surprise and then that wide smile? Oh yeah, I saw it."

"And did you see Magnum's reaction? No wonder he feels threatened. You're longer, fatter, and even better looking than he is. All the girls love you too. Diamond couldn't stop talking about how great you are."

"So what does Monte really think of me?"

"I think he likes you. Of course, he'd never tell you that. But the fact that you came through in the clutch while Phoenix is out doing god knows what. That's going to raise your stock tremendously."

"He seems kind of cold to me. Like he'd be able to commit murder at a restaurant and then finish dinner while the body is still warm."

"I don't know. He is pretty tight-lipped. But he's a family man too. His wife used to be a Vogue model. And his kids are in grade school. Some private, well-to-do school in Roswell. Seems like a lot to jeopardize. Wait. Where ya going with this?"

"Nowhere. Just making an observation."

"Mmhhm. Observation huh? Something tells me you're doing a little more than observing here. She narrowed her eyes. "Oh my god. Magnum was right. You *are* a fucking cop!"

"I'm not a cop."

It was hard to tell if she was satisfied with the answer as I could almost see her brain trying to figure out the real reason I was here. "OK then," she said. "Oh and by the way, you should go get tested again."

I cringed at the thought of Stan and his Q-tips.

Chapter 13

The internet is a stalker's paradise. All I needed to know was Monte's first and last name and the state he lived in. A people search site gave me his address in Roswell in a snap. A satellite image gave me a bird's eye view of his crib. And a mapping site gave me turn-by-turn directions. Next thing you know, I'm parked outside his house the same way the damned Feds were parked outside mine.

And what a place it was, a huge brick building with mahogany woodwork. I'd read that it had eight bedrooms, eleven fireplaces, and that it sat on two acres. It looked more like a parochial school than a residence for just one family.

I'd arrived there on a heaping helping of pure rage. Just thinking about that shiny-headed motherfucker having anything to do with what happened to Denise had me furious. My anger got me outside his place but now my brain would have to get me inside the gate.

I sat in that car for what felt like an hour, wracking my brain on how to get in there undetected. Then the perfect plan fell right in my lap. The cable guy pulled up in a white F-350.

Ever notice in the movies how when this type of shit happens, the dude just happens to be the exact size and weight of the guy who needs his uniform? Well this ain't no fucking movie.

This skinny white boy, who looked a lot like the Olympic snowboarder, Shawn White, red hair and all, couldn't have been more than five feet five. I watched as he gathered up some thick blue, red, and yellow cords, some remotes, and a clipboard with papers attached. When he went to open his door, I sprang into action.

"Hey, hey. Are you here to fix the cable," I asked as I jogged toward him. I held in the urge to call him, "Dude." His nametag read Bruce.

His eyes widened when he saw me. Then he wrinkled his eyebrows. "Uh, yeah I---"

CRACK!

I sucker punched his ass. It was lights out with one punch. Made me feel like Floyd Mayweather.

As he was going down for the count, I caught his lil' scrawny ass. I looked left and right for witnesses. The coast was clear.

I walked to the back of the van, opened the double door, and dropped him inside next to the spools of cable cords, cable boxes, and remotes. Then I shut the doors behind us.

I emerged from the van wearing dude's shirt and the nametag flipped backwards. The shit was tight. Felt like I had about 15 minutes of air left before I either took it off or succumbed to a heart attack. I checked myself in the driver's side mirror. Holy shit! It's the black Lou Ferrigno.

I looked at the nametag sown unto the shirt again. Bruce. You got that right. Bruce Banner like a motherfucker.

I grabbed the clipboard, cables, and remotes off the ground from when Bruce dropped them after I TKO'd his ass. Monte's name was on the work order.

Denise! I'm close baby. I can feel it.

I counted backwards from ten on my way to the gate to try to relieve some of the anger.

Ten. If that motherfucker did this, I'm gonna crack his skull.

Nine. This is a nice, big house. The explosion would be incredible.

Eight. Or maybe I'll just take out his wife and call it even.

Seven. Then again, since he has kids, it might hurt him more for me to axe one of 'em.

Six. Listen to yourself Ricky. You ain't no child killer.

Five. OK. No kids. But the wife is fair game.

Four. I hope these fucks don't have a dog. I hate dogs.

Three. Fuck it. I'm at the gate now. Time to put up or shut up.

Two. Got my cell phone, cable equipment…
Shit. Who am I again? Oh yeah, Bruce Fuckin'
Banner.

One. Here goes nothing…

There was a large, silver box outside the gate. It
had a number pad like a phone, a speaker, and a
small mic. I couldn't find the button marked Angry
Ass Niggah so I pressed the one that said Guest
instead.

"Who is it?" asked the voice of a child. I
couldn't tell if it was a girl's voice or a boy's
coming from the box.

"Cable guy," I said. I looked around for
cameras but didn't find any. I guessed the box and
the gate was the only security they needed. After
all, this was Roswell not Compton. I heard a loud
buzz and the gate opened.

The long walk to the front door revealed a
close-up view of Monte's acres. The lawn was
plush and green. Closer to the house were sunflower
and rose gardens.

I searched the roof and found no satellite dish.
Good thing because I wasn't about to climb on any
roof. Before I knew it, I was at the front door. I took
one last deep breath and knocked.

The door opened and a pint-sized version of
Monte answered. If I had to guess, I'd say he was
about ten years old. He wore jeans, a green Power
Ranger shirt, and all white socks.

"Are you here to fix the cable?"

"I sure am young man. Are your parents home?"

"My mom is upstairs," he said and pointed to the massive, spiraling staircase.

"Would you please go and get her? I can't come in unless an adult lets me in."

"Mom!" he shouted. "The cable man is here!"

With that, he ran towards the back of the house.

I took a moment to check out Monte's crib. The shit was nice. Baby grand piano. Furniture that looked like it came from the queen's palace. A wet bar for entertaining. It even smelled nice, like warm apple pie.

"Coming," I heard a woman's voice say from upstairs just before I heard light footsteps grow louder. She wore a blue blouse, a short mini skirt, and Go-Go boots. Watching her come down those spirals almost made me seasick.

She got to the front door. Smiled. And after I finally got a good look at her face, my soldier stood to attention.

Drop. Dead. Gorgeous.

"Hi. I'm Ella. I see you've already met Ethan. Won't you come in?"

"Nice to meet you, Ella. I'm, uh, really nice to meet you. Bruce."

She looked at the name on my shirt and then the shirt itself. If she looked at my pants, she would have thought there was a midget in there pointing to her.

"What happened to your shirt, Bruce?"

"Laundry accident. Didn't know you're supposed to wash darks in cold."

"I see," she said and laughed. "Well come on it. The problem is in one of the guest bedrooms." She turned to lead me in and towards the staircase. Damn! The girl even had an onion. It damn sure almost made me cry. Monte couldn't possibly know what to do with an ass like that.

In the stairwell, the walls were filled with family portraits. There was Monte, Ella, Ethan, and a girl who looked to be of college age. There was one of her alone wearing a cap and gown. Then there was one with Ella in a wedding dress and Monte in a tux. There was also one of little Ethan in a soccer uniform.

"The guest bedroom is right this way," Ella told me as we made it to the landing.

"I like your family portraits," I said. "You have a beautiful family." I made sure I looked her in the eyes when I said beautiful. I figured it worked because she smiled, pulled her hair over her ears.

"Thank you," she said. Then she turned and opened the guest bedroom door.

The room was decorated in all white with a touch or turquoise. There was a full-size bed with a brass headboard and footboard. It was covered in a white, down comforter. Then there was a white, five-drawer dresser, a white vanity with a huge mirror facing the bed. And finally, there was a white TV stand, which held the reason I was supposed to be there in the first place, the TV.

"There's the TV. My parents were here over the weekend and my dad just about lost it when he couldn't watch his precious History Channel."

"I see," I said while putting the multi-colored cables on the floor next to the stand.

Not only did I need some answers, I needed to stall because I don't know a damn thing about fixing cable.

"This is a beautiful room. Beautiful house too. You and your husband must work very hard to have a place like this." I searched her eyes and she looked to the floor.

"I don't work. Unless, of course, you count taking care of Ethan. On the other hand, my husband works all the time. Too much if you ask me." With that, she looked up and our eyes met. She gave me a look that said she had said too much. But there was another look I picked up on too, loneliness.

I imagined Monte coming home late from an 18-hour day of barking out instructions on a set, looking at titties and beaver and dicks and asses and fucking and blow jobs and money shots and getting home to his pretty little trophy wife and not having anything left to give. Or maybe he saw so much sex in the day that he didn't want to see it at night.

"Can I get you something to drink Bruce?" My heart skipped a beat and I turned to look behind me thinking, *Who the fuck is Bruce? And what is he doing here?* Then it dawned on me.

"Yes, please. I'll have some water."

"Hope Springs or Dasani?"

"Dasani's fine."

"One Dasani coming up. I'm just going to check on Ethan."

"Thank you Mrs. Hill."

"Please. Call me Ella. Whenever I hear Mrs. Hill, I think of my husband's first wife."

"I understand," I said. I turned to the TV and said, "Better get to this then."

"And I'll be right back with that water."

"No rush."

As she left the room, I took a peek of that onion through the reflection of the vanity mirror. Then I listened for her footsteps as they went down the stairs. "Ethan," she said. "Where are you?" Her voice became faint.

I had to move fast. If there was any evidence of Monte's involvement in Denise's death, it would have to be in their bedroom. All the criminals kept their fucking secrets in the fuck room. My heartbeat was like a Techno joint at a rave but I still managed to tiptoe out of there, into the hallway. I listened for

Ella and Ethan but heard nothing. I eased up to the first door, opened it and saw a freaking bathroom.

I listened again. Silence. Tiptoed to the next door. Opened it and saw Power Ranger posters, a race car bed, and toys everywhere. Ethan's room. Now the sweat poured.

Tiptoed. Listened. Opened. Now this looked like a master bedroom. I'll take what's behind Door Number Three, Monte.

I had no time to admire the immaculate décor in a mix of bright colors. I went straight for the dresser drawers. Found nothing but socks, folded T-shirts, Monte's drawers, and her panties. I took a handful of her silky underwear, put them to my nose, and took in one long whiff. Smelled like a combination of expensive perfume and fabric softener.

I opened the closet door and it revealed more of Ella's clothes. Leather jackets. Outfits with the tags still on them. Teddies. Camisoles. See-through negligees. I closed the door and headed towards the other closet.

I opened the door and went straight for the floor. Dudes like Monte always had a safe full of documents or a shoebox full of secrets stashed away somewhere in the closet. I used my foot to feel around inside, keeping one eye on the bedroom entrance. Sure enough, I could feel the hollowness.

Just as I was about to start pulling up carpet, I hear her from afar.

"Be right there, Bruce."

Shit!

I closed the closet door. Eased past the king-size bed, past Ella's closet and the dresser and vanity. I gave the room a once-over then shut the door.

In the hallway, I could hear Ella's delicate footsteps grow louder. So I did a Jesse Owens into the guest bedroom, got down on the floor, and started yanking out cords from the TV, cable box, and wall. Five seconds later, Ella walked in.

"Here's your Dasani," she said. "I'm having something a little stronger."

"Thank you," I said. I stood and turned to face her. She handed me the water and then took a sip of something that smelled like alcohol and papaya juice. Damn! Getting lit up in the middle of the day. Must be nice not to have shit to do all day but drink.

At first, I thought my eyes were deceiving me because there was something that looked different about Ella. Then I got it. Her blouse was unbuttoned. Make-up was touched up. She smelled just like the perfume I'd whiffed on her underwear.

"Oh my goodness," she said. "You're sweating. I'm so sorry. You must have been waiting forever for that water. Would you like me to turn up the AC?"

"No thank you misses….I mean Ella. But would you mind if I took off my shirt?"

"Please. Help yourself."

I took off Bruce's tight ass shirt and threw it on the bed. Now Ella looked like she wanted to help *herself*. Our eyes met again, this time a few seconds longer. I saw it and she saw it.

I got back down on the floor, fiddled with the cable cords like I knew what I was doing. "So what does your husband do?"

"Not me," she mumbled in what she thought was to herself. "Oh, he's a director."

"Really? Anything I might have seen?"

"Probably not. Mostly independent films. To be honest, I really don't want to talk about him."

"I'm sorry. I didn't mean to overstep my---"

"No. It's nothing like that."

"---boundaries."

"It's just that he works so much he forgets about who he's working for in the first place."

I stood up again. Grabbed her hand, looked her in the eyes, and said, "If I had a wife as beautiful as you, I'd make it my duty to remember."

She put down her drink, put her face close to mine and began to kiss me like lips were going out of style.

I grabbed her by her petite waist, moved my hands down to that onion and kissed right back. She licked my lips and shoved her warm tongue in my mouth, forcing me to taste the gin and papaya she enjoyed.

She pulled away. Turned to shut the door. Locked it and left poor little Ethan to fend for himself.

"What about your son?"

"He'll be fine. He's playing X-box. He'll be at that for hours before he even comes up for air."

I can be at it for hours and not come up for air too. And I damn sure ain't talking about video games.

She undid the last three buttons on her blouse. Took it off in slow motion. Her heaping breasts nearly fell out of her pink bra.

I took off my T-shirt and walked towards her near the door.

"Damn. Workout much?" she asked.

"Oh, I'm 'bout to show you a workout."

I kissed her up against the door and she felt my pecks then moved her hands to my ass.

I picked her up from the waist, carried her to the bed, and laid her sideways across the bed. I lay on top of her, kissed her neck, her chest, and undid her hook-in-the-front bra.

My Johnson was like concrete now. Thought it was gonna bust outta my pants and say, "Hello."

I stood and grabbed an ice cube from her libation. Laid back on top of her and rubbed it on one of her perked up nipples. Then I sucked it warm

113

again. She jerked her head back like she was cumming.

"Mmm," she said.

"You like that?"

"I do. So much."

I did the same to the other nipple. Chilled it and then warmed it with my tongue.

I put down the ice and let my hand find its way to her wetlands. Between her legs and under her mini-skirt, I touched a river that begged to be swum in. She moaned like I was doing all the right stuff.

I stood over her and smiled. Things were going exactly the way I wanted. I emptied my pockets, put some pocket change, my wallet, and my cell phone on the vanity facing the bed. I hit a button on my cell then took off my pants and boxers at the same time.

"Oh my god," she said. "My husband would love you."

I played it off like I didn't know what she was talking about. "Come again. Your husband? Don't tell me he's…"

"No. Nothing like that. It's his business. Long story."

I laughed. "Okay."

"Sometimes I need to just put a sock in it."

"I have a better idea." I reached into the drinking glass and gave her another piece of the ice.

She took off her skirt and revealed a pair of sopping wet, turquoise panties with lace trim. Then she took the ice, put it in her mouth. Took my cock, put it in her mouth. Worked it so good, I had to brace myself. Cold ice. Warm tongue. Cold ice. Warm tongue. She stroked my balls like playthings. I grabbed her hair.

"Oh shit," I said between the oohs and aahs. "Ella's got skills."

I guess her knees and her mouth were getting tired because after about six minutes of this heaven, she stood, took off her panties, and lay down sideways on the bed again.

"Do you have a condom?" she asked.

Shit! I thought I'd thought of everything. A plan to get in. Alone time to look for evidence. And my cell phone to get the inevitable on video. The one thing I forgot was a rubber. She must have seen my concerned look because she laughed and said, "Don't worry. There's some in the nightstand. "

"Thank goodness," I said. I sorted through the assortment of Trojans, Lifestyles, blues, yellows, ribbed-for-her-pleasures, and finally found a Magnum while wondering why the hell a married couple needed condoms in the first place.

"Well okay then," she said. I rolled it on.

She didn't take long to pleasure. I got on top of her, missionary style, sucked on her boobs, and eased my big boy into her a little at a time. I looked up and watched her eyes for that look when a woman realized the dick ain't gonna stop coming. Her eyes bulged out, and I knew it was time to put down the hammer.

I put my hands under her ass, grabbed it and brought her closer to me as I thrusted. Put my head down, sucked on a titty, stopped to look at her face, sucked the other one, stopped and looked, and power-pumped.

"Oh damn!" she yelled. "You are frickin' huge! You're going to make me…"

The doorknob started making noises. I looked at it and it was twisting. Then the knocks came.

"Mommy. Are you all right?" Ethan was cockblocking.

"I'm fine, honey," she said while I rubbed on her breasts, played with her nipples, and banged her even harder. "Go back downstairs and play X-box!" She yelled out X-BOX while digging her fingernails into my back. I shot my load in return.

"Smells weird in there, like when Daddy comes home from work."

"Downstairs young man," she said as I rolled off of her.

"Can I have a juice box?"

"Yes honey. You may have a juice box," she said as she put her panties and mini back on.

"Thanks Mom," he said as I heard his little footsteps get smaller and smaller.

She laughed. "I've never done anything like this before," she said and fastened her bra. All the hoes said that. I was used to it.

"Could have fooled me," I said. Put on my drawers and my pants.

"That's not what I...oh never mind." She buttoned up her blouse. "This was like something out of one of my husband's movies."

"Oh," I said. I pulled my T-shirt over my head. "I get it now. He's in porn."

"Adult films," she corrected. "He's a director."

"What's the difference?" I asked. I looked at Bruce's shirt and held off putting that tight ass thing back on.

"My husband could give you an hour-long speech about the difference. As far as I know, there is none." She looked at herself in the mirror. Fixed her hair with her hands and fixed her smudged make-up. "So are you going to be able to fix the cable?"

No but I damn sure laid some.

"Unfortunately not. I'm going to have to call in one of our specialists for this. It looks more serious than I thought it would."

"Oh. That's too bad," she said as she looked at me through the mirror.

"I didn't know your husband was an adult film director. Did he know that woman they found at Lake Lanier?"

"I have no idea. He doesn't talk about work and I don't ask him." She looked at her watch and I took my cue. "Oh dear. It's getting later than I thought." In other words, time to leave, Mandingo.

"Yeah, you're right," I said. I put on Bruce's shirt without buttoning it. Then I grabbed the cable cords and remotes. Threw the cable over my shoulder. "Just call the cable company tomorrow. Tell 'em Bruce suggested they send a specialist to fix the LX3 coaxes."

"Okay," she said. Then she unlocked and opened the bedroom door. "Thanks for everything," she said. And when she said everything, she looked straight at my crotch.

"It was my pleasure," I said. As I walked down the stairs, I repeated, "Don't forget. LX3 coaxes."

She trailed a few steps behind. "Got it. LX3 coaxes." Our eyes met one last time at the front door. We said our goodbyes and I was on my way.

LX3 coaxes, I thought to myself. I could almost hear the cable company asking her what the heck an LX3 coax was. I almost laughed right then and there when I thought of her describing "Bruce" to them.

Speaking of Bruce, I went to the van to return the cables and remotes. When I opened the van door, he was coming around, groggy and holding his face in pain. He looked discombobulated. "Oh, what happened?" he asked.

"It's best you forget what happened today Bruce." I took off the shirt and threw it at his head. "Oh," I added, "and thanks for the shirt." I grabbed my shirt from the van and walked to my car.

Just before I pulled off, I checked the video on my iPhone.

"Oh my god," she said as she stared at my eight inches of manhood. "My husband would love you."

Somehow, I doubt he will, I said to myself. Then I sped off with a satisfied grin on my face.

Chapter 14

When I walked through the lobby's front door again, Ari was waiting for me. With narrowed eyes and arms folded over his chest, he couldn't wait to lay into me.

"You son of a bitch!" he said loud enough for the entire lobby to hear. "How could you? Do you know how many nights I stayed awake working on the numbers for that Panacea deal?"

"Let's wait until we get into the office to talk about this Ari. You're making a scene." I walked to the elevator. Pushed the up arrow. Ari walked beside me, barking like a junkyard dog.

"I'm a partner in this firm Ricky. Not a damn employee, not a flunky, but a full-fledged partner. I put my own money into this firm just like you and Mike did. I want some answers!"

The elevator door opened and luckily no one was inside. We got on together and I pressed the button to our floor. Ari wouldn't let up.

"This deal was once in a lifetime, Ricky. How could you do that to Mike? Put 'em on the spot like that. He wasn't prepared. This was your baby. This was supposed to be the goddamn deal that made us rich for life."

"I can see you're angry Ari." Fuming was more like it. "But let's wait until we get into my office to talk."

"Angry doesn't begin to describe how I feel. We need to have an emergency partners' meeting right now."

"I'm fine with that," I said as I got off the elevator and made my way to the front door of our suite. "Why don't you get Mike and meet me in my office in two minutes? I'll see you there."

"You're damn right you'll see me there," he said just before I opened the door. He stomped to Mike's office and I walked the opposite direction towards mine. Two minutes later, Ari and Mike were at my door. I didn't even have time to check my e-mail.

"All right Ricky. What was so important that you had to scoot out of here in the middle of the meeting of our careers?" Ari asked.

"Have a seat guys and I'll tell you everything." Mike took a seat and I could tell his curiosity was piqued.

"I'll stand, thank you," my furious CFO said.

"That's fine. I won't beat around the bush then. Remember that story in the news about that actress found dead at Lake Lanier a few weeks ago?"

"You mean the porn star?" Ari asked. "What the hell does this have to do with..."

"Hear me out Ari. You had your say. Now let me have mine."

"Fine," he said. Mike stayed silent.

"Anyway, that EX porn star was my fiancé."

"Wait. Hold on. She was the death in the family you took off work for?" Mike asked. "Why didn't you tell me?"

"You know how I am about my personal life. I like it to stay…personal."

"Yeah but we've known each other for years. You could have told me. I mean, you were at my wedding."

"Sorry, man. I just like to keep to myself on things like my love life."

This time Ari's lips were sealed but I could tell they were bursting to say something. Finally, the volcano erupted.

"So wait a minute. I've been up day and night for months now getting the numbers right for this deal, setting up meetings, and you're out fucking porn stars?"

"I wasn't out fucking porn stars Ari. She was done with that way before we got together. And she was just one woman, a human being. I wasn't out having orgies with porn stars. We lived together. We loved each other. We were going to get married."

"Well that's all fine and dandy Ricky. But what the hell does that have to do with you walking out of the meeting?"

"If you must know, Ari, the police have their heads up their asses when it comes to the investigation. So I've been doing a bit of my own detective work on the side to get some answers."

"And?"

"And Ari, that text I got during the meeting was a lead into the case."

"Whoa buddy. I thought you left that OSI stuff behind in the Air Force," Mike said.

"I did, Mike. But we're talking about my fiancé. If something was to happen to your wife and you had the skills to find the bastard who did it, wouldn't you use those skills?"

Mike hunched up his shoulders.

"Something here is not adding up. If that's all that's going on here, why the hell were federal agents snooping around here asking questions?"

I shook my head. "That I haven't figured out yet. I know it has something to do with Denise's death. I just haven't put two and two together yet."

"You know what Ricky? I really don't give a shit! I mean I'm sorry for your loss and all but you could have hired a private investigator if you wanted to. But now you've fucked up my money, our money. I think it's time we dissolve this partnership," Ari said.

"Fine, Ari. If you want out, I can't stop you. I know you're pissed but they'll be other big deals. It might not be Panacea but hell maybe we can bring in Intel, Oracle, or IBM or something. We got Moblicity. Surely we can get others."

"No. I think you have it all wrong. *I'm* not going anywhere. It's *you* who's leaving."

Now I was steaming. I was so hot I rose to my feet.

"What da hell you mean I'm leaving? I started this business. I'm the goddamn founder."

"Tell it to your lawyer. We're all equal partners now. You have the contract. As equal partners, all it takes is a majority vote to alleviate one of the partners of his duties."

"Majority vote. Exactly. You're just one third of this company."

"And Mike is another third."

Puzzled, I took a deep breath. Sat down. Looked Mike in the eye.

"Mike, don't tell me you're siding with this hothead. You've been with me even before the beginning. Hell, you asked *me* to join."

Mike sat quiet like a church mouse for a good ten seconds and finally spoke up. "Sorry Ricky. I'm with Ari on this one. It's nothing personal but I don't think you're mentally fit to run this company anymore."

I was floored. Flabbergasted. "Mentally fit? I can't believe I'm hearing this Mike. I gave you a piece of my dream."

"Yeah but lately the dream has been a nightmare. You put me on the spot for the Moblicity presentation and then did it again for the Panacea deal. That deal was worth a lot of money to all of us. I'm sorry Ricky. Business is business."

Ari smirked.

"You know me Mike. I can bring in more business. That was just the tip of the iceberg."

"It's too late now," Ari interrupted. "We want you out of here by the end of the day."

And just like that, the meeting was over. Ari walked to the door. Mike stood up and joined him.

I could not believe these motherfuckers had just voted me out of my own company. I should have been smarter about that contract.

I knew Ari was an asshole. But Mike? Didn't see that one coming at all. Out by the end of the day. Fuck it. At least now, I would have no distractions in finding out who killed Denise.

Tabitha Corning, the manager of the IT prospecting department was standing outside my office after it all went down with Ari and Mike. I'd forgotten about our standing meeting. Dressed in an all-red business suit, with a low-cut blouse and tight business pants, she looked professional but sexy. This was one of many coaching sessions we had scheduled. When it came to a division of duties, White Mike handled the day-to-day stuff like dealing with unhappy customers and hiring new staff. Ari was the money and finance guy. And I was the big picture guy. But because I could sell gasoline in hell when it came to telemarketing, I also took on the duty of coaching to pass on some of my knowledge.

Sometimes she'd lean her five feet eight frame over my desk to show me something on the computer. She might have been trying to show me something else. Or she'd smile her cute smile. It never occurred to me in other meetings that she might be flirting. After all, I was damn near married and totally in love with Denise. Tabitha was decent looking too. But with her interests in country music, hunting, and all that outdoor shit, that last thing I thought she'd ever want was a black man, CEO or not.

I wanted to suplex Ari's ass. But I said to myself, *this is your company Ricky. You need to calm your ass down and get back to business. You can deal with this Ari situation later.* I started counting backwards from ten to one and then led Tabitha into my office.

"Mr. Stunt," she said with a twang. "I'm having some problems coaching reps who get hung up on right after the prospect says he's not interested. Do you have any ideas?" She flashed a smile, uncrossed her legs, and leaned forward. Damn! Maybe she *did* want me. Maybe I could work off this anger.

Oh I got some ideas all right.

"Mr. Stunt?"

"Oh, yes. Ideas. I've got a few. First of all, they should make sure to call one level above first and try to get a referral. That way, if they get the prospects on the phone they can let them know that they spoke with their boss first. They should be all ears then."

"Good idea Mr. Stunt." She clicked her ball point pen and began taking notes on a small, yellow notepad. "Anything else?"

"Yeah. They need to be smiling when they make calls. That pleasant voice should cause prospects to be a little nicer about hanging up on our reps."

"Sound nicer and smile," she said and wrote. "Got it."

"One more thing. They might try emailing the prospects first and then calling them later that day. These IT folks are all about the digital, email, texting, social media. A lot of them hate talking on the phone. But if you get their attention by the means they're most comfortable, they should respond more positively."

"Excellent! That makes perfect sense. You always have the right answers Mr. Stunt. I could just kiss you," she said as she stood.

"How 'bout a hug instead?" I asked while the bulge in my pants said I should change the H in hug to an F.

She came around to my side of the desk and stretched out her arms as I inhaled her Eternity for Women. I squeezed her tightly, let her feel the boner in order to see if she wanted it. After the hug, I saw the look in her eyes and the long pause as if she was lingering around for something else. I was ready to bend that ass over my desk and tear that pussy up. Make her sing "Yeehaw" loud enough for the food trucks outside to hear her. I started to go in for a kiss and she was meeting me halfway. But then I thought about where I was and what could happen if I got hit with a sexual harassment suit or if one of the partners caught us on top of everything else. Instead of kissing her, I hugged her again.

"I, um, I have another meeting in about five minutes. You let me know if you need anything else."

She looked like a fat kid who just missed the ice cream truck. And she looked at my pants like they were a Bomb Pop. "OK, Mr. Stunt. I will," she said. Then she left the room and closed the door behind her.

I locked the door and had a little talk with myself.

What's wrong with you Ricky? This porn shit got you trippin' man. You can't be screwing the employees. Real life is not a skin flick. Get it together!

I walked to the sink in my office and turned on the cold water. Splashed it on my face. Pulled down my pants and let my dick run under it. I had to get control of myself. Focus. I had to deal with this Ari and Mike shit and find Denise's killer. It was time to let my real brain, and not the one in my pants, take charge again.

Then my iPhone buzzed in my pocket.

911. Need you at the studio in an hour. Can u make it?

The timing was perfect.

On my way...

Five minutes later, I was in my Beemer, doing 80.

Chapter 15

By the time I arrived on the set, the superstar they called Penis Williams was off to the side. He was dressed in a fuzzy turquoise robe and sitting in a leather chair. The dark brother looked like he needed Samuel L. Jackson to come and yell "Rise up" to his dick.

"You're right on time Ricky. The girls are waiting." She took my hand and led me to the set and whispered, "Are you ready?"

"I'm cool."

"Have fun," the deep-voiced superstar said. At least he had a good attitude about it.

The ladies were sitting on the bed, side-by-side. Their robes were loose enough to see that they were naked underneath. Had the nerve to be having a conversation like normal people too. The sista, who had long curly hair, big Mila Kunis-like eyes, dark brown skin and a tight little body was talking about how her trifling ass ex was not paying child support. The snowbunny listened like a psychologist before adding that their kids should get together for a play date. She had legs that went on for days, dirty blonde hair, a spray on tan, green eyes, and an Ultrabrite smile. Her open robe allowed for a peek at those huge silicone-implanted boobs. Upon seeing me, that Ultrabrite smile turned to an outright scowl.

Monte was messing around with some camera equipment, talking to three or four set guys. I thought about his wife and smiled to myself.

"Who the hell is *this* Melissa?" she asked as if I wasn't in the room.

I'm the dude that's 'bout to fuck you into next week.

"Now Vivian Viagra. Is that any way to talk to people?" Melissa asked. Vivian folded her arms across those monstrosities. "This is the stunt. His name is Ricky. Now play nice."

Apparently, the black girl liked what she saw as she almost tripped over Vivian to introduce herself.

"I'm Pamela Pussy," she said and extended her hand.

"Nice to meet you, Pam." I shook her hand. Her smile widened.

"Great. Another stunt dick. Has he even been tested Melissa?"

"Of course, Viv. You know everyone gets tested weekly. Quit being such a diva."

"Yeah Viv," said Pam. "I'm kinda looking forward to this one."

"Whatever."

"Ricky, follow me to the dressing room and I'll give you a rundown of the scene," Melissa said. "And you'll love this," she said as if I was trying to make a career out of this shit. "The film is called Anus versus Mars."

"Don't keep us waiting too long," Pam said.

"Pay no attention to Miss Vivian," Melissa said as I unbuckled my belt, unzipped, unbuttoned, and let my pants and drawers fall to the floor together. Her face turned red and I could almost hear her heart palpitating. "She's one of our biggest stars. Monte flew her and Pam in from L.A. Plus she's making an appearance at Magic City while she's in town. Viv is kind of a prima donna. "

"Is that the new word for bitch these days?"

"I guess you could say that. Don't worry though. Pam is a sweetheart. She'll keep it balanced out there. Plus it looks like she really likes you."

"Charmed, I'm sure," I said with sarcasm. "What do you need me to do?" I asked. Although with a title like Anus versus Mars, I had a general idea. But when Melissa told me everything that was about to go down, it took everything in me to keep a straight face.

Back on the set, Vivian was naked and on all fours at the edge of the bed. She rolled her eyes at the sight of me, despite my fully erect Louisville Slugger. But that freak Pam looked like she was ready for me to hit a home run. And that naked and athletic-looking body was looking good. All she needed was one of those foam hands with the index finger sticking up.

Damn right, I'm number one. And you're about to find out.

I was determined to wipe that smirk off Vivian's face. I manhandled her by the waist. Wasted no time and put half my dick up her ass while Pam tongue-kissed her mouth and played with her fake breasts. Her crapper was loosey-goosey. As I looked down on her back, I imagined her ass with that old McDonald's sign hanging over it reading: OVER 1 BILLION SERVED.

Screw this bullshit. I gave her the full eight.

"Oh shit!" she screamed.

Pam peeked around Vivian's body and watched as I pounded in and out of that ass with everything I had. Tried to knock her smug ass to the next room.

"Save some of that for me," she said. Then she kissed Vivian on the chest. Then the navel. Eased her way down to the pussy and started making slurping and mmm mmm good noises like she was shooting a soup commercial. Before I knew it, she put her hands on my balls. First, she caressed them gently and then she cupped them. Fingers. Cupping. Fingers. Cupping.

Soon they flip-flopped but not before I gave Vivian a now-you-know look and she gave me a now-I-know-look. I stood on the edge of the bed. Now it was Pam's turn. Her ass was a lot more plump and jiggly than Vivian's flat one. Wouldn't surprise me if she could make it clap. And by the time I was done with her, the look on her face told me I was due for a round of applause anyway.

In the dressing room, Melissa told me to be sure to come on Pam's ass. Something about the script calling for the white on brown contrast as if porn directors were some kind of artists. But my jizz had a mind of its own as it shot not only onto her Jell-O-like ass but up into those curly black locks and down her sexy back.

I started to head to the bathroom when Monte asked, "Where ya going?" He pointed the lens to the floor.

"Melissa said the scene ended with a blow job?"

"Yeah, and…?"

"I was just going to wash up."

"Wash up?" Monte asked while the women giggled.

"Fucking amateur," Vivian said as she got down on her knees and shoved my shit-covered, nut-covered dick in her mouth.

Monte lifted the handheld and started rolling again.

"Mmm. Chocolate *and* vanilla," she said between slurps.

I tried not to lose my lunch before Monte yelled cut. But the scent of sweat, semen, a bowl of diarrhea, and the thought of her tasting it all like a shish kabob was more than I could take. I hurled a colorful display of pink, brown, and green slime all over Vivian's head. Now she was *really* a dirty blonde.

"Fucking amateur!"

Chapter 16

Two days later, by the time 6:00 p.m. rolled around, my eyes were screwy from staring at my computer screen. I combed through the Buck Nekkid website. Googled names and looked at the video of me and Monte's wife a million times. Now I had some leverage against his ass. If the interview tactics I'd learned in the military didn't make him talk, I'd bet my money that the video would.

I went back to Grady Memorial again to see my old friends Ugly Face and Stan. They looked at me like I was some kind of lunatic when I showed up for another round of torture. When we finished up, Beatrice handed me a pamphlet about the dangers of having sex with prostitutes.

You have no idea.

I made a mental note to just go to different hospitals next time. Northside next week. DeKalb Medical Center the next. That way it would be all new to the staff and they wouldn't judge me for it.

Just as I was fantasizing about the many ways I would beat the shit out of Monte, I got a text from Melissa.

Stunt Dick 9-1-1. Shooting on location @ The W. Room 535. How soon can u get here?

About 45 minutes.

Make it 30 if you can.

I'll do my best.

Man this shit was starting to get old. And rush hour was a bitch at this time of day. So I took a different route, up I-85 to 141 then south on 400. During rush hour, this was always faster, even though it was 15 or 20 miles farther.

Since Melissa's text caught me off guard and my anger was getting the best of me, I had forgotten that Monte and the rest of them had never seen my BMW. This luxury would be a dead give-away that I was not some talentless clown trying to make it in the world on the strength of my dick.

I would have to find a place to park far away from the hotel and hoof it. An hour after receiving the text, I was knocking on the door of Room 535.

Melissa greeted me at the door wearing a black, see-through negligee, a black bra and matching panties.

"What took you so long?' she asked. She pretended to be mad but I could see her smile after she pretended to pout.

"What's going on here Melissa? Where's Monte and the other actors?"

"Come in and I'll explain."

I walked in and the smell of cherry-scented candles and perfume lit up the air. She shut the door, locked it with the deadbolt and the chain.

"I have a confession," she said. "There's no shoot here tonight. Unless, of course, you want to make one for your eyes only."

The trick she'd used to get me there had me steaming. Here I was thinking I was about to get some sweet revenge on Monte's ass and all this was a booty call.

"Now don't be angry with me Ricky," she said. She eased her way up to me until her face was close to mine. "I just haven't been able to get that afternoon at my apartment off my mind. You made me feel *so* good." She went to touch my face but I grabbed her wrists and pulled them down to her belly.

"Hold on Melissa. That day at your apartment was just a sex thing. I don't have time for no love shit."

"Who said anything about love?" she said. "I was just hoping for a friends with benefits type of thing. Who knows? Maybe we might even get to know each other and actually find something in common."

"And what ever happened to no recreational sex? The last thing I need is a Viagra prescription in order to make a buck."

"Please. You're a young and virile man. I don't think you'll have any problems in that department." She broke away from my grip and put her hand on my crotch.

138

"If I do this for you," I said while moving her hand off my cock, "you've gotta do something for me."

She took a step back, looked herself up and down and said, "I thought I was doing something for you." The look I gave her brought her back to reality. "Fine," she said. "What is it you want?"

"Get me a one-on-one with Monte."

"A one-on-one with Monte?"

"Yeah. He won't talk to me. At least not for very long. And that whole barfing deal didn't help either."

"And why do you need to talk to him so badly?"

"You just let me worry about that."

Melissa turned away from me and walked towards the door. I walked up behind her. Let her feel me rising on her backside. It didn't take long for her to make up her mind. "Okay, I'll do it."

"In that case," I said and then kissed the side of her neck, "I'll do *you*."

"Take off your clothes," she said to me like she was the one in charge.

"Why don't you take 'em off for me?"

"Ah hah," she said. "Aren't we becoming a superstar?"

I say nothing. Just smile. Then she reached for my belt. Got down on her knees. I stroked her hair as the buckle jingled and buttons came undone.

With my pants around my ankles, she kissed the bulge in my tight black boxer briefs. Then she looked up at me as if her eyes were seeking permission.

A little late for that.

At a snail's pace, she pulled down the drawers. Palmed my ass cheeks like a life preserver and got her lips up close to my dick. She shook her head, laughed, and said, "Amazing."

Damn right, I think just before she kissed the tip. Licked it. Devoured it. Tried to take it all in which was damn near impossible. I closed my eyes. Enjoyed the pleasure. Then I took off my shirt while she worked her magic lips, tongue, and hand.

Just when I feel like I was about to erupt, she stood to her feet. Then she wiggled out of her lacey black panties. Let them fall to the floor before stepping out them. She walked backwards and eased her butt onto the bed. I joined her.

"I have a surprise for you," she said. She started feeling under a big fluffy pillow for something. But I'd learned by now to let nothing surprise me in this world. Still my mind wandered. Double-sided dildo? Anal beads? Her idea was less imaginative, two pairs of furry handcuffs.

"Oh hell naw," I said. "My people were in shackles long enough. I ain't about to wear none voluntarily."

"Don't be silly Ricky," she said. "They're for me to wear." She handed me the things and laid flat on the bed.

The king-sized sleigh bed seemed built for them. I took the cuffs. Kissed both her legs from knees to thighs. She squirmed with delight. I kneeled over her, knees on either side of her belly, dick pointing to her face as if it was accusing her of something wrong. I grabbed her wrist. Chained it to the post. Same with the other. Now her eyes were saucers.

"What are you going to do to me?" she asked and grinned.

"The same thing I do to all the bad girls."

"And what's that?"

I answered with more kisses on her neck, and then her chest before ripping the lingerie and bra away from her breasts. "Let's just say, I won't be sparing the rod."

I laid on top of her. Used my tongue. Worked circles around her breasts before sucking the nipples. My hands and mouth took turns with each of them. She smelled of something cherry. I looked at her shackled wrists and got excited with power. I grabbed her legs. Pointed her knees towards the ceiling fan. Then I rubbed my balls on her belly. My cock too. Like slow motion, I dragged it to her Mohawk bush, on her clit, and into her heaven.

"Oooh," she moaned before I grabbed her shoulders for leverage. I stroked hard. I stroked in. Out. Clockwise. Counter. She moaned with every movement I made, alternating between oohs, aahs, and yeahs. The headboard was not so sturdy. It reacted to every stroke too, banging up against the wall. Thwat! The rhythm was like the bass of a House music jam. Her vocals added to the mix.

Thwat." Oooh." Thwat. "Aaah." Thwat. "Oooh." Thwat. "Yeah."

I turned her lower half to the side as the cuffs wouldn't let her turn her whole body. Then I sucked her titties and fucked her at the same time. My hands rubbed her back and grabbed her ass. Her torn lingerie flapped on her body like a flag in the wind. Cherry and sex funk filled the air.

Before you knew it an hour passes and her eyes rolled in the back of her head. The four little words escape her lips. Body shook like an epileptic. Comforter a pool of stickiness. Her pussy was a pulsating pleasure pen. I powerstroked it hard and fast. It sucked me in like a Venus Fly Trap. My wad could no longer be contained. I prepared myself for the money shot, even though the cameras weren't rolling. Pulled myself out of her and jizzed all over her stomach before grunting out loud like a Neanderthal.

Afterwards, she said to me from under the sheets, "Now I'm starting to get it."

"Get what?" I asked half sleepy from the sex.

"The questions. The interest in Magnum and Monte. Now it all makes sense. You're the reason Denise had become so happy. Whistling even while Monte degraded her and yelled out insults. Oh my god. You're Denise's big love."

At that point, I didn't know if I should level with her or come clean about my reasons for wanting to know more about Monte. My gut was telling me I could trust Melissa but my mind was telling me she could be involved herself.

I studied her face and wondered if she'd go running to Monte and open her mouth. But the only thing I saw on her face was jealousy.

"I'll take your silence as a yes. Well listen," she said. "I'll tell you this. That bald bastard was certainly there the night Denise was killed. So was Stacy Prince and his cronies. If I were a betting woman, I'd put my money on one of them having something to do with it. Maybe both of them."

That feeling of rage started to take over. "How do you know? Were you there, too?"

"Heck no. Execs only. I'm just a lowly lighting director slash personal assistant. I was out at The Varsity with some old friends that night. Monte's the big director. And Stacy Prince, as you probably know, is Atlanta's king of porn, AKA executive producer and bankroll for all of Buck Nekkid's movies. He's the reason you're holding all those fat checks."

"And let me guess. He just happens to own a yacht he sails on Lake Lanier."

"Hmmph. Guy is so rich, he probably owns Lake Lanier too. But if I were you, I'd steer clear from Stacy Prince. I've never met him personally but the guy has a nasty reputation."

"If he's so awful, why do you work for him?"

"A girl's gotta eat. I'm sure he's not the first or the last asshole producer in porn or mainstream for that matter."

"I need you to do me a favor Melissa. Don't breathe a word of this to anyone."

"Don't worry Ricky," she said and nudged me under the sheets. "Your secret's safe with me. It's a shame though."

"What do you mean?"

"You could have been a real superstar in this game. A very rich superstar."

Chapter 17

True to her word, Melissa set up a meeting with Monte. A couple of days had passed since I'd told her where I wanted to meet him and what time of day.

"I told him I found a cool location for a shoot and that he should meet me there at 7:30," she said.

The day before, I'd done a little shopping to prepare for the meeting. Nothing special. Just some pliers, matches, gasoline, rope, duct tape, and a 38. Besides the gun, these were just ordinary household items. But in my OSI days, we used them to get the truth out of terrorists and assholes.

I arrived at the abandoned warehouse in Decatur fifteen minutes early. The building used to be a small manufacturing firm that made car parts. During the recession, it was one of the first casualties. 212 jobs gone like that. 212 families scrambling to make ends meet. I picked up one of the dust-covered signs off the floor. It said BUY AMERICAN.

"Hello. Melissa, are you here?" I heard his voice from a distance. "It's me Monte," he said. His voice grew stronger.

I hid behind a beam until he was close enough to reach out and touch.

"Melissa," he shouted. "Where are you?"

I pulled out the .38 and jumped out from the beam like the Boogeyman.

"No, motherfucker. It ain't Melissa."

"Stunt? What the hell? Where's Melissa? What kind of shit is this?"

"It's time I start asking the questions around here. Now sit yo' ass down over in that chair over there." I pointed with the weapon.

"Now wait a minute here Stunt. I demand an explanation."

I pistol whipped him across the head. "You ain't demanding shit," I said as I watched him stagger to his knees. "Don't make me say it again. Take yo' ass over to that chair and sit yo' ass down."

"All right. All right," he said. Held his hands up while saying it. "I'm going to the damn chair."

I smiled. He rubbed his head where I'd hit him. When he sat in the old wooden chair, I grabbed my duffle bag from behind the beam. I reached in and pulled out the rope. Kept the gun pointed at him.

I walked over to Monte and pulled his hands behind him. Tied a strong knot behind the chair.

"Is that really necessary?" he asked. "Whatever this is about, I'm sure we can straighten it out over a beer."

I remained silent like someone had read me my Miranda rights. Got more rope. Tied his legs to the chair.

"What is it? Do you think you're being underpaid? You want a guarantee that I'll make you a star? What?"

"You wanna know what this is about Monte? All right. I'll tell you. This is about a woman named Denise Dupont."

"Double Dee? Wha-what about her?"

"Whatchu mean what about her? You were there the night she was killed. I know this for a fact. What I want to know is, what did you have to do with it?"

"Don't tell me you're a cop, Stunt. If that's even your real name."

"Do I look like a cop?"

"Actually, you kinda do. In case you didn't know it, I have friends in high places in the department."

I bitch-slapped him. "I ain't no cop, you dumb ass. I *am* a pissed off motherfucker though."

Monte spit blood on the floor. "Well if you're not a cop, why the hell do you want to know about Denise? That was before your time with us."

"Because she was my woman. The woman I was going to marry! Now she's dead. And if you don't answer my questions, you're going to be joining her."

Monte pulled my hoe card. Laughed out loud like he was at a Richard Pryor concert.

"So let me get this straight. You fell in love with a porn star, duh, strike one. You come to my set posing as a stunt dick to do your so-called investigation. Strike two. And now you commit a federal offense by kidnapping me and expecting answers? Strike three."

"I didn't kidnap anybody," I said. "You came here on your own volition."

"Hello? You have me tied to a chair. I'm not free to leave at will. Therefore, that's classified as kidnapping."

"You know, I've had about enough lip from you," I said. I walked to the duffle bag and pulled out the duct tape. I tore off a large piece and taped it over his mouth.

"Before I leave this warehouse tonight, you gonna tell me what I want to hear Monte or you won't be leaving at all."

I grabbed the pliers from the duffle bag and his eyes grew wide. It was starting to feel like the Middle East all over again. All of a sudden, it was as if I was back there where it all started...

I'd heard lots of rumor about Colonel Jack Stone before I had entered his class on counterterrorism. Among the rumors, his father worked for J. Edgar Hoover and was one of the agents who helped bring him down. Another one was just after he'd graduated from West Point, not only did the

CIA, FBI, and each branch of the military recruit him hard but so did the NFL. At just over seven feet tall and with the body of Adonis, he was given the nickname The Bonecrusher during his football glory days. But the rumor that stuck was that the character Keifer Sutherland played on 24 was based on his life. They didn't even bother to change the character's first name.

Colonel Stone would often tell me I was one of his top students. But I wondered how many other officers he said that to.

Stone taught me everything I know about torture. Taught me how the simplest household cleaning products could be used to my advantage. Once he showed me how a Diet Coke in the microwave would blow like a little grenade. He even taught me how to read body language, eye movements, and how to tell if a suspect was lying.

"Most liars look down and to the left when they lie," he said. "Or they reach back and touch the back of their neck."

During the war, we took a C-130 to Oman on a TDY. These temporary duties often became permanent ones if the military required it. There had been rumors of a local asking our airmen questions about the number of troops on the ground and about when the next planes were coming in. Those were red flags. One airman reported this to OSI, and that's when they called us.

Turned out the so-called local was a Yemeni terrorist passing as a dry cleaner in the tent city. Colonel Stone took the lead. It had to be a hundred degrees in the desert yet he turned off the A/C in the tent. He had the thirty-something brown man tied to a chair. His mouth was duct taped and his hands were behind his back. Before Stone asked even one question, he took a switchblade and sliced the back of the Yemeni's ankle with it. He let out a blood-curling scream, even through the duct tape. After the screaming stopped, the interrogation began.

"Remove the tape from his mouth, Captain Stunt." I did as ordered.

"Now why is it that you're asking American service members about troop movement and airplanes?"

"It was just, how-do-you-say, curiosity. My boy is fan of military. Wants to move to U.S. one day," he answered in thick Middle Eastern accent.

I kind of felt sorry for the guy. Wondered if his story would check out. Only problem was, he was looking down and to the left when he answered.

"Did you see that captain?"

"Yes sir."

"Just like I taught you in training."

Stone kept going. "We have photos of you and a known al-Qaeda member at several different locations. The photos were taken via satellite." He reached into his fatigues. "Would you like to see one?"

"It's true," he said. "I have cousin who is al-Qaeda. I am try to get him to leave. Start new life."

Stone winked at me. He knew he had him. I knew there was no such photo or he would have shown it to me.

"Then how do you explain the recordings we have of your voice planning to shoot down U.S. planes?"

The colonel was playing a hunch. And it paid off. In a snap, the Yemeni man showed his true colors.

"Fuck you American pigs," he yelled. Spit in the colonel's face. "Soon you will all pay for killing innocent Muslims with your bombs."

That was all Stone needed to hear.

"Captain Stunt," he said. "Would you give me a few minutes alone with our friend here?"

"Yes sir," I said. Then I left the tent and headed towards the Army and Air Force Exchange tent. No more than a minute later did I see a sight that will forever be with me. Colonel was smiling wide and walking. He was calm like five minutes after busting a nut. The tent was on fire. And the screams could be heard throughout the entire Tent City.

"He told me what I needed to know."

"And?"

"And I had no further use for him."
War is a dirty business.

"What happened that night with Denise?" I asked Monte.

He shook his head. So I went behind the chair, pried open his fist and went to work on his pinky. I heard him screaming through the tape as the pliers crunched down on the bone.

"What happened that night with Denise?"

He shook his head again. It was déjà vu only this time it was the pinky on his right hand. "Damn Monte," I said. "I don't think you'll ever wear a pinky ring again." He screamed through the duct tape and then tried to scoot the chair away from me.

"Where you going Monte? We're just getting started. You ready to talk?"

Monte nodded. It's amazing what a couple of broken fingers can make a man do. At least, that's what I thought.

I ripped off the duct tape and he spit right in my face. "Go fuck yourself Stunt. I'm not telling you a goddamn thing!"

I was cool. Put the tape back over his mouth. Wiped the spit and blood off my face with my sleeve.

"Oh you want to play with liquids, huh? We can play with liquids."

Stunt

I picked up the bright red gasoline can and
poured all two gallons on him like it was salad
dressing and he was a big, egg-headed Cobb. "Let's
see what you have to say now," I said and pulled
out the box of matches.

Instead of screaming, I heard him mumbling
through the duct tape. But I'd heard that before. I
wasn't about to be spit on again. Instead, I took out
a single match and struck it against the box. I
smiled at the beautiful blue-orange flame. "Ready to
talk now?"

He shook his head.

In the Air Force, we used to call types like
Monte loyalists. Loyalists would take torture all day
and never budge if they believed in the cause. Some
would even die for a cause they believed in.

I blew out the match then removed the thick,
gray tape from his mouth.

"Yes," he said. "I knew it. I knew you weren't
the murdering type. You might not be a cop but
you're not a murderer either. I can see it in your
eyes. Now will you please untie me from this
raggedy chair and let me go home?"

It was clear he was unstable. So I pulled my ace
in the hole.

"Guess you wanna get home to the wife and
kids, huh, Monte?" I pulled out my cell.

"Look, Stunt. You gave it your best shot. Let
me go and I won't tell the cops about our little

incident from tonight. And by the way, you're fired."

"I heard you got a beautiful wife. Little one running around looking just like you."

"Whatcha getting at here?" he asked. He spat some more blood on the floor.

"Oh nothing. I just heard you had a beautiful family, that's all. Of course, I couldn't believe an old chrome dome like you could have a beautiful wife. So I had to see for myself."

"What? Stunt, if you so much as put a finger on her…"

"Oh, I put more than a finger on her all right. In fact, I made a nice little video I know you'll like." I put the phone to his face and said, "Action bitch!"

The video started right when she was sucking me off with ice. "Do you know who that is?"

"You son of a bitch. Turn it off. Turn it off!" He turned his head away from the screen. His face was red and he was fighting back tears.

"You sure Monte? The best part is coming up."

"Please," he said. "Turn it off."

I hit the POWER button on my phone.

"Let's make a deal Monte. You tell me what I want to know about what happened to Denise and I won't post this video of me fucking your wife up on YouTube."

In a flash, the smart ass comments, the sarcasm, and smug attitude vanished. Now he looked concerned.

"All right. I'll tell you what you want to know. But you didn't hear this from me."

And boy did he tell it. Told me all about how Stacy Prince had connections high in the police force. About how Prince took pleasure in killing her himself and how he'd flung her body out to the lake from his yacht like a piece of trash. I knew the name, the producer Melissa talked about.

"And you didn't do anything about it?"

"I couldn't. Prince is untouchable and is certainly not a man you want to fuck with. He has half the Atlanta police force on payroll. Even plays racquetball with the chief. On top of that, he's got the two largest, meanest looking bodyguards you've ever seen. He never goes anywhere without them."

"Stacy Prince huh?" How do I know you're not lying just to cover your own ass?"

"Believe me. Telling you about Prince puts me in more danger than you ever could."

"So why tell me at all?"

"Let's just say there are some things more important than saving your own ass."

Yeah, like your wife's rep.

"Don't worry. I'll get you your video and all the copies as soon as this checks out. So you know him. How do I get to Prince?"

"Um, unless you're into getting your ass fucked, you don't."

"Say what? Stacy Prince is gay?"

"As gay as they come. He asked me to introduce him to Magnum. Next thing I hear, they're freaking butt buddies."

I knew that motherfucker was gay. Magnum Come Lousy.

"Can you get me a meeting with him?"

"Yeah but only if I tell him you're a raging homo."

"All right. Tell 'em I'm a homo."

"What? Are you nuts? You try to fuck with Stacy Prince and you will end up getting fucked by Stacy Prince."

"You let me worry about that. I know how to handle myself. What's the phone number?"

Monte told me the phone number. I punched it into my phone and held it to his ear. Told him if he set up a meeting, the video was his and he'd never have to see my face again.

When the conversation was over, Monte told me that Prince would be in Vegas in a few weeks at an annual adult film awards show and convention. I was to meet him there alone.

I cut Monte loose after he'd set up the rendezvous at Prince's hotel. He was staying at the Red Rock.

"One more thing," I told him. "I don't want to hear any shit about you giving Melissa a hard time for setting up our little meeting. If I do, my dick and your wife's face will be online like that." I snapped my fingers.

"Don't worry," he said.

Monte ran out of the warehouse. He was happy to be alive.

Stacy-fucking-Prince. Yeah, I knew who he was alright. Now I was ready to get in his ass, and not the way Magnum did either.

Part II

Chapter 18

After my violent night with Monte, I pulled up to my condo. As I parked my ride, I noticed those same two Feds in that black Buick parked two houses back. But tonight, instead of sitting there staking me out, they jumped out and made their way towards me in my parked car.

They finally found their balls, I thought as the hard shoes clicked on the concrete. I got out of the Beemer and started walking to my front door. They caught up and met me there.

"Excuse me, Richard Stunt?" the older one asked. He must have been the senior agent. His forty-something looking pale face was far more weathered than the other one's mug. He had a high and tight, old-school haircut. He wore a wedding ring. And his shoes were square on the end. He carried a briefcase.

"Who wants to know?" I asked.

"Federal agents. May we enter the premises?" He showed his badge. It said Gary Larson over a shiny gold star. I gave them a once-over in their all black suits.

I thought about talking to them right there outside my door. But knowing my nosey neighbors, I'm sure a few of them were peeking through the blinds and trying to listen in.

"Sure," I said. "But I'm kind of tired. I had a rough night."

"We won't take too much of your time," said the younger one. He looked as if he was fresh out of college. Had a Justin Bieber haircut, deep tan, and he wore expensive Italian shoes. No wedding ring.

I opened the door, flicked on the light, and led them to my little kitchenette set where Denise and I would talk just before work. Before she would kiss me goodbye. Sometimes those kisses got so good that they turned into more and I'd end up giving Ari and Mike a lame excuse for running an hour late. And every time it was worth it.

I thought about offering them a drink but that would have given them a reason to stay longer than they had to.

"Mister Stunt, I'm Agent Larson and this is Agent Bunn. We won't beat around the bush," said the older one.

"I appreciate that."

"Do you know of a Stacy Prince?" Just hearing the name almost made me blow my top.

"Heard of him. I don't know him personally. Why?"

"The United States government has had Mister Prince under surveillance for over two years."

"Damn. Two years? My tax dollars hard at work. Must be some serious shit."

160

"Yes, it is. We believe Mister Prince is one of the largest distributors of child pornography in the country, maybe the world."

I rose from my chair. "Wait. Hold up. Did you say child pornography? Kiddie porn?"

Larson opened the briefcase and pulled out a yellow folder with the words Stacy Prince written in dark magic marker. He handed me the folder.

I wanted someone to burn out my eyes after I saw the images. Grown ass men having sex with girls who hadn't even developed breasts or even pubic hairs. They looked afraid. They looked like they were in pain. And there were other pictures too. Pubescent girls with pubescent boys. Pre-teens posing for the cameras wearing nothing. I felt my stomach twist up in knots. If Prince was responsible for this, he had no soul.

"Yes sir," Bunn said. "He uses a modeling agency as a cover. Excelsior Modeling Agency recruits unsuspecting kids and their parents through radio and newspaper ads promising stardom."

I thought about the older woman who had her teenage daughters in the lobby trying to be models.

I played it cool despite the pictures. "Interesting. So why don't you just arrest him?"

"It's a bit complicated," Larson said. "You see, during this investigation we uncovered the involvement of several Atlanta Police Department officers. Turns out, he's used his money and influence to turn half the force into his personal security force."

"Yeah. That might go as high as the chief of police," Bunn added.

I sat back down. I wanted to go pour myself a strong drink. "Well that's all interesting but what does this have to do with me?"

I'd asked the million dollar question. The agents gave each other a knowing look then looked back at me.

"Come on, Stunt. We know what you've been up to. Known since the start."

"Up to? What the hell are you talking about?"

"I won't beat around the bush. Did you ever notice how the night those officers stopped by the night your fiancé was discovered they didn't ask you any hard questions? Or did you notice that no detectives ever came to interview you?"

"Come to think of it, I did."

"And given your background at OSI, I'm sure you know that if the wife or the girlfriend is murdered, the number one suspect is…"

"The husband or the boyfriend," I finished. "So why haven't I been questioned or detained?"

"That's because this has always been a federal investigation, and we believe Prince is responsible for the murder of your fiancé, Denise Dupont."

Just like the government to show up a day late and a dollar short. Tell me some shit I don't already know.

"Really? What's your theory?"

"We have reason to believe she either stumbled across some of these pictures or either overheard something she wasn't supposed to hear about the children's pornography business. And when Prince found out he…"

"I get it," I said.

"We're really sorry for your loss," Bunn added.

"So sorry you follow my ass all around Atlanta and not tell me a damn thing about what you know?"

"That was nothing personal. We just had to get an understanding of who we were dealing with," the young one said.

"So you poke around my place of business and make my partners suspicious. Is that how the FBI works these days?" They looked at each other but said nothing. "Anyway," I said, "what am I supposed to do with this information?"

"Well, Mister Stunt. We have reason to believe that you have the inside track on Prince's operations."

Shit. There it was. They really did know what I was up to all along. Probably tapped my phone or researched my internet history through the web provider. I glanced at my laptop and tried to play dumb.

"Inside track?"

"Yes. And we're not here to judge your methods. In fact, I think we can all help each other out," Larson said.

"And how would we do that?"

Bunn said, "We know about the kind of work you did in the area of conflict during the war." If I didn't know any better, I could have sworn I saw hero worship in his eyes.

"You guys really did your homework huh?"

"Sure did. A man with your background working on the inside of Prince's operations could be the key to bringing him down."

"Well, why don't you put one of your agents undercover and get the bastard?"

"Oh, we wanted to," Larson said, "but the Bureau can only go so far, if you know what I mean."

Yeah, I knew what he meant. Uncle Sam couldn't get no pussy to solve a case.

He continued. "But a private citizen such as yourself…"

"OK. I get it. Well, let's just say I have this inside track you're talking about. Why do I need The Feds' help?"

"We could provide weapons, wire taps, protection…"

"Rules and regulations," I added.

"True," Larson continued. "But if you get him our way, it'll be legit. If you play vigilante, you might end up in jail or worse, dead."

"But we know you can handle yourself," Bunn added.

Not wanting to show my hand, I said, "To be honest, I don't even think I can get to him. I mean, I'm just one guy. If he has the whole Atlanta Five O protecting him, what can one man do?"

"I'll tell you. We've been staking him out. Studying his habits. We discovered that every Friday he hangs out at a dance club called The Tool Shed."

"That gay bar in Stone Mountain? Oh hell no. I ain't going nowhere near that place. That's way too many third legs near my virgin ass. No thank you." Just the thought of something entering my exit hole almost made me shiver.

"It's the only place he feels relaxed enough to let down his guard. Leaves his bodyguards behind."

"Probably doesn't want any witnesses to him getting juked up the ass."

"Could be. But you could wear a wire. Get him to talk. With your help, he could end up spending the rest of his life in federal prison."

The federal pen? I thought. *He'd probably enjoy it too much with his choice of knobs to polish.*

I'd much rather see that motherfucker pushing up daisies.

"So what do you think Mister Stunt? Are you in?"

"Kiddie porn huh?"

"Disgusting isn't it?"

Damn right it is. I'm going to have nightmares about those pictures for weeks.

I thought about the times Denise and I would take long walks in the park and would stop to watch the kids play. They'd chase each other playing Tag, laugh in high-pitched voices, and push each other on the swings. Denise and I would talk about having kids together. They'd be cute little bi-racial babies with her hair and beauty and my brains and sense of humor. Not only did Prince steal the innocence of children just like the ones we saw at the park, but he also took away our future.

"Count me in," I told Larson.

"You won't be disappointed," he said and then smiled. "Let's meet tomorrow morning."

A few minutes later, I showed them both the door with the promise of meeting at Starbuck's before noon.

I thought about what Larson said. *You won't be disappointed.* Oh, but ya'll will be disappointed because when I get my hands on Prince, I'm sending his ass straight to hell.

The next day, we meet at the Starbuck's up on Sugarloaf Parkway. At ten thirty a.m., the place was jammed pack with caffeine addicts. That included yours truly.

They were waiting for me at a table in a dark corner in the back. The older one summoned me as I walked in and I went that way right past the stand of coffee beans, mugs, and gift cards. I saw a group of teenagers who looked like they were studying for an exam together. There was also a guy with a laptop. A quick glance at his screen showed he was on a job board, looking for employment. Damned economy ain't no joke.

I cut to the chase. "All right fellas. How do we do this?"

"Prince will be at the Tool Shed tonight. All we need you to do is to wear a wire, strike up a conversation with him and see if he'll talk."

"And what if he doesn't?"

"In that case, sniff around the people he hangs out with. Ask them some questions. See what they say about him when he's not listening." He sipped on a tall drink from a white cup.

"Okay. And yesterday, you mentioned you'd have some firepower for me."

The younger one reached down under the table and pulled out a briefcase. "I think you'll find everything you need here."

Jet Black

I opened the case and there was a handheld
Glock, a wire, and a throw-away cell phone. "Nice
Glock," I said. "But what if they have a metal
detector?"

"They won't. We already cased the place. No
metal detector. No pat down. I guess they all feel
safe amongst their own kind. Now the wire goes…"

"Trust me," I interrupted. "I know how it
works."

"Of course," he said. "We'll just be a few
blocks away, in case anything goes down."

"I can't believe I'm doing this shit," I said. "A
fucking gay bar. Guess I'd better go shopping for
some tight ass pants."

Chapter 19

After my meeting with the federal agents, I went straight to Discovery Mills Mall. I found me a pair of pants so tight it looked like they were taking my blood pressure. When I looked in the mirror, I could see an outline of my cock in the crotch of the pants.

Look but don't touch motherfuckers.

That same day, I heard a loud knock on my door at four in the afternoon. I looked through the blinds and discovered a sexy little sistah dressed in a business suit. I opened the door.

"May I help you?"

She smiled when she looked at my face. Her eyes widened as they found their way to my crotch. "Are you Mr. Richard Stunt?"

"Yes. Who wants to know?"

"You've been served," she said and handed me a manila envelope.

"Oh it's like that huh?"

"I wish it wasn't," she said looking back down at my pants again. "You have a nice day."

When she walked away, I shut the door and tore open the envelope. It was just as I'd expected. Ari and Mike were suing me for breach of contract and officially asking to settle on dissolving the partnership. I read through a lot of the legal jargon up to the point about the non-compete agreement. If I wanted to start another telemarketing firm, I'd have to wait a full year as to not compete with them. Compete against my own damn firm. The agreement stated that if I signed, I'd walk away with one hundred grand. If I didn't, I could end up with nothing. As serious as it was, I had to put it in the back of my mind and focus on The Tool Shed.

I fired up my laptop and brought up some images of Stacy Prince. I had to hand it to him. Unlike Monte, his face was hardly ever photographed. No IMDB credits. No About Town photos. Just a few pics from a couple of years ago. Snapshots at an adult film awards banquet. Motherfucker was the color of midnight. Big dude, too. Had to be about six feet five and husky. Looked like he knew his way around a gym.

Damn, I thought. Why do it have to be a brother?

Now I was going to have to add to the statistics of black-on-black crime when I killed his ass.

Ten o'clock couldn't come fast enough. At 10:01 I was standing in line at The Tool Shed, tight pants and all. Glock in my sock. Behind me stood a couple of drag queens. One of them, a Latino, was obvious with his broad shoulders and five o'clock shadow. The other one, a light-skinned brother, could have passed for a woman had it not been for the Adam's apple.

Mr. Broad Shoulders smiled at me. I nodded as if to say, "What's up?" My knees were like Weeble Wobbles.

When I reached the front door, I spoke into my shirt. "I'm at the door. 'Bout to head in."

They had the nerve to be playing some decent music up in there too. While I was expecting a continuous loop of *It's Raining Men* or *YMCA*, it shocked me to hear the latest jams by Beyoncé, Usher, Young Jeezy, and all the other chart-topping artists. I forked over the twenty dollar cover and made my way into the bar.

"No sign of Prince," I said to my chest. The wall at the bar was mirrored. I looked at myself and thought, *What the hell are you doing here?* The bartender made his way to my stool. He was a little guy with a baby fro and a tight shirt that revealed muscles. My guess was a Napoleon Complex.

"What's your pleasure girlfriend?" he asked in a high-pitched falsetto.

"Scotch on the rocks," I countered in my deepest, manliest voice.

"Oooh. A real man," he said. "I'd like to get *your* rocks off."

"Uh, no thanks," I said. If I was light enough I would have turned five shades of red. "I'm waiting on a friend."

"What a lucky friend," he said. "One Scotch on the rocks coming up."

I imagined the federal agents parked a block away in that Buick laughing it up at my expense. Why couldn't one of them assholes do this undercover bullshit?

Napoleon Complex came back with my drink. I studied it for the date rape drug before taking a sip. Tried to relax. Get a feel of the place.

This place was wild. There was a shirtless brother in a cage wearing leopard print pants. I wouldn't call what he was doing dancing. More like screwing the air. Then there were some couples on the floor, touching and grinding on the flashing dance floor. They reminded me of when I was a teenager in Detroit and one guy would say "Fuck you," and the other one would say, "Two dicks don't stick." But from what I was witnessing, apparently they do.

The drag queens tripped me out the most. Some of them were so convincing, if I saw them on the street, I would have tried to holla at them. They had hips like women, asses like women, and even managed to hide their Adam's apples. I could see myself bringing one home to some Crying Game shit.

I was cool until I saw the dudes making out. Tongues going every which way but loose. Hands moving at the speed of light grabbing a handful of ass or balls or both. I threw up in my mouth a little bit.

Then I saw him. Wanted to reach into my sock. Pull out the ten millimeter. End it. End *him* right then and there. But he had a posse with him; among them, Magnum's sorry ass.

"I have a visual," I said into the wire. *I have a visual*, I thought to myself. Felt like my OSI days again. But now I had to make sure Magnum didn't get a visual on me or my jig would be up.

As they came through the door, I turned to face the mirrored wall. I angled my face towards the bar so that Magnum wouldn't see me. But I kept my eyes on the mirror. Then I saw it for myself. They passed the bar and headed for the back room, which looked like it was probably for VIPs. As they passed, Prince palmed Magnum's ass. Then they turned and kissed like they were at Inspiration Point and this was fucking Happy Days. If I had my way, it was going to be the last of Stacy Prince's happy days.

When they disappeared into the back room, I followed. As I approached the door, the posse greeted me. And this was no Wal-mart greeting either. This was a take-another-step-and-we'll-melt-a-cap-in-your-ass greeting.

"May I help you?" a huge white guy who had a body like Arnold Schwarzenegger asked. He revealed his piece holstered on his side. It didn't take a rocket scientist to see he was an off-duty police officer.

"I was just looking for the bathroom," I said.

"Bathroom's over there," he said. Pointed towards a corner on the other side of the club.

"Oh, thanks. Is this the VIP?"

"This is the none of your business."

"My bad. My bad," I said. I backed away from the door, keeping my eyes on The Terminator.

Now I was salty. Larson's and Bunn's intel was shit. Prince didn't need his bodyguards as long as he had half of Atlanta's finest watching his back. Good thing Monte had already set up a one-on-one with Prince in Vegas at the Adult Film Awards. And that one-on-one would be my one and only shot. I wasn't about to let their bullshit detective work blow it for me. No wonder they'd been following him for two years.

If I was going to get to Prince, I was going to have to do it my way. But first, I needed to take a trip home to Detroit.

Chapter 20

When my plane landed two weeks later, it felt surreal. I couldn't believe I was standing in "The D" once again. I hadn't been there since before college, before the military, and before all this mess with Denise.

When I left Detroit, I hadn't planned on returning. Left all my old friends behind. Not that I was running from anything. Just didn't like what the city was becoming, crack houses, corrupt mayors, and murderers. I was ready for a fresh new start. Told my parents that they could always come to visit me in college, on base, and later in Atlanta if they wanted to see me. They even managed to make it down a few times. That was way before Denise, though. Before I started The Phone Room.

As much as I loved them, I wasn't sure I'd have time to visit them. I was in town for a reason, to talk to my old buddy Luther Peyton from my OSI days.

Luther and I met during a tour of duty in Iraq, during the war. When he discovered that both of us were from Detroit, we hit it off lickety-split. I learned that not only was he the smartest electronic gadgets guy in the Air Force, but he could keep you in stitches with his jokes.

After the service, he decided to give it a go as a full-time comedian. And it was going well for him back home until he had to deal with the business side of things. Club owners cheated him out his fair share of the cover when he packed the house. Some of them, ex-comedians themselves, got jealous of his success and limited his stage time. He even had a sitcom producer make him an offer as a writer on a pilot. But it only lasted six weeks.

When he called me out of the blue to tell me his plans, I was more than happy to help.

"How they treating you down in Hotlanta?"

"Better than the Air Force did."

"I hear that Captain."

"Captain. Man that brings back memories."

"How they treating you at home?"

"Now you can't call it home if you don't come to visit every now and then. We gonna have to get you up in here. Have you visit the projects to remind you of what The D is all about."

"Um, I'll pass on that. Wouldn't mind some Pizza Papoulis or some Steve's Soul Food. They don't know nothing about that down here."

"Man, Steve's shut down a while ago. Whatchu talking about anyway? Ain't you in the south where soul food was invented?"

"Yeah, well tell that to the restaurant owners 'cause they don't know nothing about that."

"See that's where you going wrong. You gotta find you a fine sistah that can burn. And make sure she ain't too skinny because if she too skinny, she ain't eating right."

"Oh, is that right? So how's the comedy career going?"

"It's cool. I'm about to open my own comedy club. These owners be trippin'."

"Yeah. Nothing like having your own."

"Actually, I was hoping you could help me out."

"I'll do my best. What do you need?"

"About ten grand."

"I see you still got jokes."

"I do but I'm dead serious bro."

"And what do I get for my ten grand?"

"You get ten percent ownership in one of the hottest new comedy clubs in the Motor City."

"All right man. Sign me up. So what you calling this club anyway?"

"LMFAO."

"That's perfect."

After renting a Honda Pilot at the Avis in the airport, I headed straight to the freeway. Jumped on I-96 then took I-94 downtown. While driving on Jefferson, I passed signs for the new casino and the signs for the tunnel to Canada. A flood of memories came. Hanging out at Hart Plaza during the jazz festival and the African-American fest. Driving up to Windsor and hanging with my boys. Finding those easy Canadian girls who couldn't get enough of some brothers from the U.S. Smoking weed and getting laid at a chick's house whose name I forgot the next day.

Next thing you know, I'm parked in front of LMFAO. The sign lit up in bright blue and red lights. There was a billboard that said, "Coming next week, Mike Epps." I looked at the name of the club again. Knowing Luther, he probably literally had them laughing their fucking asses off in there.

The lobby walls showcased signed headshots of some of the greats: D.L. Hughley, Kevin Hart, Steve Harvey, and Cedric the Entertainer.

The hostess was a cute little thing. And when she asked for my ten dollar cover and said, "There's a two-drink minimum too," I smiled as I forked over the cash even though technically I was a ten percent owner.

I eased in and rushed to a seat I found in the back. Luther was on the stage just finishing up a set, looking like a big brown M & M with his beer belly and circular frame.

"And I thought racism was supposed to be over since we got a black president. Man, even Google is racist. I saw this white gang jack my car one day. So after I called the police, I Googled white people stole my car. Then Google suggested," he said using air quotes, "do you mean black people stole my car?"

Stunt

The audience were dying laughing. He continued.

"A brother just can't get a break. I can't even get a break at home. Nobody told me marriage was just legalized prostitution. I asked my wife, 'You wanna do a little something-something tonight'? She said, "I don't feel sexy without my hair being done." Luther used a high-pitched voice when he mimicked his wife. "I said, well how much is that gonna cost? She smiled and said, "two hundred fifty dollars. I said damn! For two hundred fifty dollars I can have a three-way with two crackheads and get a new suit at K & G."

Now the audience was in tears with laughter. He had them just where he wanted them.

"And don't get me started on the kids. I swear those little crumb snatchers have boner detectors in their brains. They can be outside for hours, laughing, playing and hollering. Let me try to get a little lovin'. Beep beep beep. Beep beep beep. Warning! Warning! Daddy is trying to get his freak on," he said like a robot. "Quick let's get home before he reproduces. Less Christmas gifts. Hurry! And as soon as I put in it, I hear the front door slam. Mommy, Daddy, we're hungry. I said to my wife they might be hungry but I'm starving. And what does my wife say? Now baby. You know you can't let your boys starve. Let me get dressed and fix 'em something to eat. I'll be right back. I said baby they

179

almost grown. Them boys five and seven years old." The audience was in stitches. "When I was seven, I was cooking eggs, bacon, frying chicken and even hunting my own venison. You making them soft. Luther come on she says. I said I'll be right back. Now deep down I wanna believe my wife but I know in my heart that once she leaves that room it's going to be me and a jar of Vaseline five minutes later."

Luther pretended to stroke himself. "Freaking two hundred and fifty dollar weave. I could have hired three midgets to do this shit for fifty dollars each and some shoes with lifts."

The place was filled with laughter, including my own. And that last joke had me thinking about little Ethan trying to open the door on me and Monte's wife. The shit was funny because it was true.

"Hey that's my time tonight. My name is Luther Peyton. You guys have been a great audience. And be sure to take care of your waitresses tonight." Luther headed off the stage and handed the mic to the emcee. His act made me hate that I only caught the tail end of it. He always cracked me up, even during wartime.

I rose from my table and headed towards the stairs where he was leaving the stage.

"Give it up for Luther Peyton," the emcee said. The audience clapped loud. "Come on ya'll can do

better that that. The nigga said he ain't paying me if
ya'll don't clap louder." The audience laughed at
the emcee's joke, stood up, clapped louder and even
whistled.

"Coming to the stage is a woman who needs no
introduction," the emcee said.

"Nice show," I said.

Luther was busy looking down when he said,
"Thank you, brother. I'm glad you enjoyed it."

"You should be writing for TV," I said.

That got his attention. He looked up and saw
my face smiling back at him. "Captain Stunt!"

"Captain Peyton." Luther gave me a big bear
hug.

"What the heck brings you to Detroit?"

"Can't a brother visit an old friend? I see
you're still killing it on the stage."

"What can I say brother? I'm living the dream.
Come on. Let's go back to my office and talk.
Whatchu drinking?"

"Scotch and soda."

"Tenisha," he said to the dark-skinned sistah
with dreads behind the bar. "Two Scotch and Sodas.
Can you bring 'em back to my office please?"

"Sure Mister Peyton."

Luther opened the door that led to his office. It
wasn't the grandest thing. A wooden desk with
snapshots of his wife and two boys. A leather chair
behind the desk. Two metal folding chairs in front.

Off to the side were boxes of restaurant equipment. Shot glasses. Drink stirrers. Napkins.

"So this is what I own ten percent of, huh? Not too bad Luther. Not bad at all. Full house and everything."

"I do all right. Have a seat Ricky." I picked up one of the metal chairs and sat. He sat in the leather one behind his desk. Then there was a gentle knock on the door.

"It's open," he said.

Tenisha entered. "Here are your drinks, Mister Peyton. Do you need anything else?" She placed the drinks on his desk and I stole a peek of that round mound of a backside. She had the kind of ass you get from eating just the right amount of buttermilk biscuits.

"That's all for now," he said. "Thank you."

"You're welcome sir," she said. She walked to the door and closed it on her way out.

"Like I said, looks like you're doing all right for yourself."

We both laughed. "What? Tenisha? That girl's in college at Wayne State."

"But that ass would make a brother want to go back to school."

"And that ass would have a brother like me paying alimony and child support for the rest of his life. No brother. Me and Rhonda still in love. My chasing tail days are over. When you gonna settle down and get married?"

"Actually, that's what I came to talk to you about, in a way."

"You gettin' married? Mister Playboy himself?"

"Not exactly," I said. "I was going to though."

"So what happened?"

I gave Luther the Cliff Notes version of what happened with Denise, what was going on now and my plan. Ex-porn star. Undercover stunt dick. Melissa. FBI. Stacy Prince. Child pornographer. Pretending to be a homo just to get to him. When I was done, he drank his drink in one gulp.

"I'm speechless. I-I don't know what to say. You know I'm sorry for your loss brother. Is there anything I can do?"

"I was hoping you would say that."

"Because if it's about the ten grand, I can have that back to you with interest tomorrow."

"Thanks, Luther. But what I need from you is far more valuable than money. I need you to summon those old OSI skills."

Luther looked at the snapshots of Rhonda and the kids on his desk. "That was a long time ago Ricky. My life has totally changed since then."

"It's cool man. I wouldn't ask you to go to the front lines or anything. I know you got a family.

Hell, it's rough enough trying to run a business in downtown Detroit."

"Damn right it is. Young bucks tried to rob the place once. But you know me, I had a few gadgets installed for such an occasion. One dude touched the register in the wrong spot and got tazed. Sent 25,000 volts of electricity up his ass. Old boy's partner tried to get away but when he touched the door knob it blew up and sent three fingers flying through the air with it. I ain't never seen nobody flip me off like that. I guess word got out because nobody has tried to rob the place since."

A light bulb seemed to flash over his head. "Oh, I got it. I could make a mini-high-voltage bear trap and fit it for your rectum. And when dude tries to give it to you up the ass, it'll shock the shit out of his dick and then snap it right off."

"Man, I hope it don't come down to some nasty shit like that. But damn, I gotta do whatever it takes." I grabbed my drink and downed it.

"Same old Stunt. Still sweating over getting juked in the butt one day?" He laughed and looked at my empty glass. "You want another one?"

"Maybe later," I said while ignoring the other question. "I was thinking something different though."

"All right Ricky. So what did you have in mind?"

"Something a little more gentle, like an undetectable wire."

"Oh man. Is that all? I can do that in my sleep." He pulled out a laptop from his desk drawer and opened it. "Check this out."

I looked at the screen. He had video and audio of every crevice of the place. He zoomed in on the front door, the lobby where the wall of fame resided, the waitresses talking, and even Tenisha as she made change at the register.

"Damn, brother. Paranoid much?"

"Paranoid my ass. This is The D. Ain't no such thing as being too careful."

"Like they say, you can take the brother out of M.I.T..."

"...but you can't take M.I.T out of the brother," we said in unison and then slapped hands.

"How soon do you need the wire?"

"In a couple of days. After that, I'm off to Vegas."

"You got it brother."

"I'm not going to have to stick the thing up my ass am I?"

"No," he said and then laughed. "But it'll be in the neighborhood."

"I figured as much."

I stood to leave.

"Aw man. Can't you stay a little longer? Stay and watch the rest of the show. Let's catch up on old times," he said and then stood. Then he walked to the front of his desk.

"Not this time. I still haven't gone to see my parents yet."

"I can dig that. Be sure to tell the deacon and Mrs. Stunt I said hello. And swing by here before you head to the airport. I'll have your wire ready." He shook his head. "A freaking murderous child pornographer. You need you about twenty roughnecks straight outta the joint to go with you and fuck his ass up. You want me to make a call?"

"Naw man. I got this," I said. "Later."

"Later," he said. He slapped my hand, gave me a half hug, and I was out.

Chapter 21

I must have circled the block four times before I finally parked in front of my parents' house. Down 8 Mile to Middlebrook and up 10 Mile and over to Route 39. But it didn't take all four times to realize the neighborhood had been run down. The boarded up houses, crack addicts, and drug dealers revealed that the first go-round. By the time I drove around the fourth time, the dealers were taking notice and looking nervous.

This wasn't the Detroit I grew up in. The Detroit I grew up in was proud of its black mayor not ashamed of him for trying to get his freak on and getting caught through texting. It was a city that held its head up high because the basketball team won back-to-back championships. I remember when the grown-ups drove around with their brooms in honor of sweeping the Lakers. The Motor City was proud of its auto workers too, making all those Fords and Chryslers for the world to drive. We even had our fair share of local celebrities in the form of Anita Baker, David Alan Grier, and the stars of Motown.

When I told people in the Air Force I was from Detroit, it earned me instant street cred. Little did they know that I was just a nerdy little deacon's kid, at least until I got to high school and discovered girls and they discovered me. But even though I was doing it, I didn't let it distract me from getting good grades, getting a full ride scholarship and balancing a bevy of Sunday school, three worship services, and Wednesday night Bible studies.

Talk about a 180.

I rang the doorbell. The light over the peephole darkened. "Junior. I can't believe it. Richard, it's Junior," my mother said. She got so excited that she forgot to let me in.

"Hello? Ma? Are you going to let me in?"

My father opened the door instead. "The prodigal son has returned," he said. "Well don't just stand there, come on in son."

Dad gave me a big hug and then looked me eye to eye. Mom followed suit. Her face pressed against my chest when she hugged me. "What a pleasant surprise. Why didn't you tell us you was coming? I would have made your favorite dinner."

"It was sort of a last-minute thing. More business than pleasure."

"Business?" my dad asked. "On a weekend? What kind of business you…"

"Now Richard. Don't you start with all the questions. Let him at least get in the door."

"It's okay, Ma. Anyway, I'm only in town through tomorrow."

"Oh Lord. Now you know we ain't gonna be on this earth forever. Would it kill you to spend a couple of weeks with your old mom and dad?"

"Next time Mom. I promise. In fact, why don't I send for you and Dad next month and you can stay with me as long as you want."

"You know I can't leave my church for that long. The reverend needs me."

"Ain't that what you have other deacons for?"

"Oh don't get him riled up about them other deacons. Boy come on over here and have a seat," she said as she motioned towards the sofa.

The couch looked exactly like it did when it was brand new. That's because they kept that shiny and uncomfortable plastic over it. The plastic reminded me of high school and in an instant I was a student at Renaissance High all over again.

Mom and Dad had gone away to a religious convention for the weekend. While they were gone, I invited the head cheerleader, Darnesha Robinson, for a visit. We sat on this very same sofa when things started getting hot and heavy. First base. Second base. Third base. Just when I thought I was sliding home, Darnesha slid off the couch and bumped her head on the coffee table. There was blood everywhere. It turned out to be nothing more than a small contusion but you could have fooled me back then. She left me home alone with a hard on and a hard time trying to get the blood stains out of the carpet. I spent the weekend worried about what my dad would do to me if he found out I was trying to fornicate right in his living room.

Though the couch looked the same, I wished I could have said the same about my parents. Mom was completely gray and was shrinking. Age spots and wrinkles had taken over her skin, too. But her loving spirit was still there.

And Dad had put on at least 50 pounds since I saw him last. And it was all in his gut. When I was in high school, his hair and mustache was a sea of pepper with a bit of salt mixed in. Now the reverse was true. Plus, Dad had his share of wrinkles as well.

"So Junior," my mom said. "When you gonna bring me some grandbabies?" As of late, it was my mother's favorite topic.

"Yeah, son. I read all about Atlanta. Heard it has the most black gay men in the country, a regular Sodom and Gomorrah. I hope they ain't done turned you..." He punctuated the sentence by stretching out his palm and moving it side to side like Fred Sanford.

"Oh hell no," I said and then watched my parents' faces almost explode. "Sorry. I mean heck no."

"Watch your language, Richard Stunt junior." I was sixteen years old all over again. I held my head down in shame.

"Well when you gonna at least bring home a nice girl for us to meet? You know, Bernice Watson's daughter is still single."

"Who? Constance? That girl was kind of a piggy. Just because we went out on that one date you've been trying to get us together ever since."

"But you should see her now, Ricky. She lost all that weight. Got her hair fixed up in them there whatdoyacallem extensions. And she ain't got no babies. Gotta good job, too. A real big shot at the library."

"That's great for Connie but I just got out of a relationship. Actually, that's what I wanted to talk to you two about."

"Seems like you always just getting out of a relationship," my dad said.

"Yeah but this was different, Dad."

"When you gonna learn that this running around fornicating…"

"Dad, we were engaged." Those magic words put an end to the beginning of a 30-minute sermon.

"What happened, Ricky?" my mother asked.

"She passed away."

"Oh my Lord," she said. Raised one hand in the air. Looked like she was about to catch the Holy Ghost.

"What was it, son?" Dad asked. "Cancer? Heart disease? You know they say that's the number one killer of African Americans."

"It's a bit more complicated..."

"What? Asthma? Blood clot? Don't tell me it was that HIV."

"No, Dad. She was murdered."

"Murdered!" they shouted in unison.

"Told you it was complicated. Is it okay if we change the subject? I'm still getting over it. Plus it's late and I don't want you up all night over this."

I could tell that it was killing them not to hear more specifics. But with Ma's high blood pressure and Dad's previous heart attack, I knew that telling them more could really kill them.

"Of course, Junior," Mom said. "We just wanna make sure you're all right. You hungry? I got some sweet potato pie in the refrigerator."

"That sounds great, Ma. But you take it easy. I'll go and get it."

The plastic on the couch crunched and squeaked when I rose. Then I walked into the kitchen and opened the fridge. It gave me a few minutes to think.

Though I grew up in a household of religious tolerance and acceptance of all races as equals, I think my parents assumed that I'd marry a black woman. What a trip it would have been if they'd met Denise.

I removed the Saran Wrap from the pie and took a long whiff. It brought back a million Thanksgivings and Christmases with uncles, aunts, and cousins. Sweet potato pie was my favorite dessert. But not just any sweet potato pie, my mom's sweet potato pie. That and a glass of milk was almost better than sex.

"Can I get you anything?" I asked from the kitchen.

"No we're fine," my mom answered.

When I returned, their eyes were glued to the eleven o'clock news. It reminded me of when I was a teenager and they had this fine reporter on Channel 4. I used to spank it to her big time.

"Same ole. Same ole," my dad said. "Murder, crooked politicians, and unemployment."

"You ever thought about moving? Maybe retiring and heading down to Florida? It'll probably be nice to get away from this crime and the cold winters up here."

"You can't run from the devil. All you can do is ask the Lord to cover you," Dad said.

There was no talking to my dad without it becoming a religious conversation. So I changed the subject.

"Ma, this pie is so good. You put your foot in it." I wolfed it down like I'd never eaten it before.

"Thank you, baby. If you came home more often, I could make pies for you all the time."

"Yeah and I'd probably weigh 300 pounds if I did."

We all laughed at that one.

"But I bet that Connie Watson could help you keep it off. She got herself a personal trainer. You should call her." The woman was relentless.

"Maybe next time, Mom."

I woke up the next day in my old bed, my old room. Back in the day, I'd wake up to a poster of Toni Braxton staring down at me. Ooh the things I wanted to do to her.

I even had an old school poster of Rick Mahorn and Bill Laimbeer posing as the Bad Boys of the Pistons. They were known as the dirtiest players in the league. But nobody in Detroit cared because they brought home championships.

I spent the rest of the day visiting my old hangout spots. Chandler Park. Belle Isle. Mexican Village.

I headed back downtown. Played a few slots at the Greektown Casino. Had myself some deep dish at Pizza Papoulis. Later that night, I took my parents out to dinner at Fishbone's for some seafood and gumbo. On the way home, we passed the Joe Louis fist and Dad went into his speech about the history of black athletes and how hard it was for them to enter white-dominated sports back then.

It felt good to be home again. I almost forgot about all the trouble with Denise and the whole Buck Nekkid Productions stuff until I received a text from Luther telling me the wire was ready.

On my way to the airport, I stopped at LMFAO. Luther instructed me on how to use the wire.

"Just place these two wires under your ball sack. Stick this part on the bridge between your scrotum and your butt."

"Looks like little suction cups on the ends. What if I sweat?"

"No problem. You could spray a high-powered hose on it and it won't come loose."

"That'll work," I said.

"Hey, Ricky, man. I've been thinking about what you said with this whole situation and I've been wanting to ask you something."

"Yeah, man. Go for it."

"This Melissa chick. You ever think she might be steering you wrong because *her* hands ain't so clean?"

"I kind of thought that at first. Whatchu thinking?"

"Peep this. She knew your girl personally. She ain't put up no fuss when you asked her to set up the meeting with this Monte dude. And she says she was nowhere near that boat when your girl was murdered. How can you trust that though?"

"You got a point there. I thought about it. Just didn't see a motive."

"Yeah, I thought about that, too. You probably right. Unless she got something to do with that kiddie porn crap, too."

"Hey, man. Nothing surprises me in that industry. Good looking out."

"Just looking out for my boy."

"Thanks, man. This means a lot to me. And about that ten grand, consider us even. I don't need to be no ten percent owner of a comedy club in Detroit anyway."

"For real, Ricky? That's cool brother. You sure I can't call up some hard brothers from the hood to go to Vegas with you?"

"Naw, man. I'm straight." We slapped hands.

Next thing you know, I'm back at Detroit Metro airport. I reached into my carry-on to get my ticket and found a little green Bible. "Figures my dad would do something like that." But if anybody was going to need a Bible, it was going to be Stacy Prince when I finally got to him in Vegas.

Chapter 22

My plane had touched down in Vegas in the early afternoon. But with the time difference, it felt like 5:00 p.m.

The airport was filled with slots and sluts. Some weirdo-hippie looking guy handed me a deck of cards. Each card showed the picture, measurements, and special skills of a different hooker. But I don't pay for pussy. Pussy pays me. Now I saw why this was the perfect setting for the Adult Film Awards. After the fans got all worked up, they could pay for a prostitute and live the fantasy. Legally.

I'd dressed like an everyday Joe for the trip. Blue jeans, black T-shirt, and some black sneakers. Didn't want to stand out.

I hailed a cab and had the driver take me to the Nevada Convention Center. When we arrived some thirty minutes later, the first thing I noticed was the jam-packed parking lot. Then there were the women, most of them gorgeous and almost naked. Finally, I saw the huge white banner with black lettering outside the building saying: WELCOME ADULT FILM AWARDS. I paid the driver and made my way towards the entrance.

Through the glass double doors, the air conditioning hit me hard. And judging by all the high beams I saw in the place, it had hit the women pretty hard, too.

"Welcome to the Adult Film Awards," stated the bubbly brunette dressed in a business suit. She stood and handed me a logo-filled plastic bag for swag.

"Thanks," I said and took the bag. "Where's the show?"

She pointed. "If you go to your left and walk past the big brown kiosk and make a quick right, you'll be right there. Or better yet, just follow the crowd."

And what a crowd it was. There were men who could easily be truck drivers, school teachers, lawyers, or even college nerds. Many of them showed no shame in taking photos with their favorite adult film stars at vendor booths.

The booths were everywhere. They sold DVDs, double-ended dildos, soundless vibrators, flavored condoms, and even pussy. Most of the vendors were women, who would yell a "Come here," or "Let me show you something," from their seats. I ignored them and made my way to the theater. When I arrived, there were only a few seats left. I eased into one of them in the back of the auditorium that could easily seat a thousand.

Among the sea of faces were Vivian Viagra and Penis Williams. They were seated near the stage and chatting it up.

A Hispanic woman with long hair, a cute smile, and huge breasts smiled at me from two rows up. "What are you doing after the show?" she asked.

"I'm not looking for a date."

"You know," she said. "I'm not a pro."

"Yeah, but I am." With that she turned her head back towards the stage.

Then I saw him. Dressed to the nines in a dark blue Calvin Klein three-piece suit. I'd seen one in GQ just like it and it cost nearly two thousand dollars. It made me think of the filthy way he earned his money. The kids. Then I thought about Denise. I ripped the logo-filled plastic bag.

The house lights went down and a huge applause started. "Ladies and Jerk offs," the voice said. "Welcome to this year's Adult Film Awards." Cat calls joined the applause.

An hour and a half later, I had just witnessed the weirdest awards show I'd ever seen. They'd given out awards like, Best Blow Job, Best Three Way, Best New Cummer, The Pearl Necklace Award, Best Vocalist, Best Girl-on-Girl, Best Money Shot, the Up-the-Keister Award, and Producer of the Year.

I'd never heard of most of these so-called winners who thanked directors, first loves, spouses, smarmy Phys Ed teachers, and co-stars. Vivian Viagra won the Up-the-Keister award. Big surprise.

And for the second year straight, the Producer of the Year award went to Stacy Prince.

"More like producer of child pornography," I mumbled. As he stood on the stage in his expensive suit, I thought about how glad I was that I did things my way and made Monte set up the date in Prince's hotel room.

I eased out the auditorium the same way I eased in. Fought through the aggressive vendors and asked that brunette who greeted me to call me a cab.

In my room, I prepared myself for the moment I had been waiting for. I'd already let Larson and Bunn know my plans. Told them if they wanted to get the son of a bitch, they'd have to do it my way. I told them about the wire Luther made and how I was going to get a confession out of that bastard. All they had to do was record it and show up with a gang of Las Vegas-based feds when the time was right and arrest his ass.

Freakin' two year investigation. If they fuck this up, they should just turn in their badges.

Chapter 23

The twin towers stood on either side of the room's entrance. One of them even recognized me.

"Dick Stunner," he said. "Pleasure to meet you. The name is Gary. And that's my brother, Larry." He stuck out his hand. "Mister Prince is expecting you."

"Thank you, Gary," I replied and shook his hand. The grip was damn near close to cutting off my circulation.

"Man, I saw a sneak-peek of your clip for The Audacity of Hoes. Whoo. You sure gave that Sugar Tits a run for her money. You make Magnum Cum Loudly look like an amateur."

"What can I say?" I said and hunched up my shoulders.

"Hey, brother," he said. "Sorry we have to do this but we gotta pat you down before you go in to see the boss. Nothing personal."

"No problem," I said and stretched out my arms and legs.

Larry patted me down from ankles to underarms. Chest, back, and stomach. Thighs, calves, and shoes. "He's clean," he said. Then he gave his brother a sly smile.

Gary opened the door. "Go right in, Mister Stunner."

"Hmmph," Larry added.

I knew what that gargantuan brother was thinking. Thought I was there to pull a Magnum and cum my way loudly to the top.

The sight of Prince in his expensive business blue and white pinstripe suit with a white button-up shirt and the top two buttons undone was surreal. I'd tallied in my mind all the ass I had to tap: Karen, Melissa, Diamond, Sugar Tits, Vivian Viagra, Pamela Pussy, and Monte's wife just to get to him. Then I thought about Denise and how he just flung her out to the lake like a piece of trash. I balled up my fists and prepared myself to kick some ass.

"Well, if it isn't my future superstar himself, Dick Stunner." Hearing him say that ridiculous name I'd chosen for myself made it sound even dumber.

He strolled from the suite's bar area to the living room to greet me. The closer he got the more I wondered why he even needed bodyguards like the twin towers. Man had to be at least six feet eight and built like Ray Lewis. I had to look up to him.

"Nice to finally meet you, Mister Prince."

"Please. Call me Stacy." He reached for my shirt and started undoing the buttons. I wanted to puke.

"Can a brother at least have a drink first?"

"Don't get it twisted, "he said letting his femininity seep out. "I'm just making sure you're not wearing wire."

When nothing but my bare chest was revealed, I said, "Satisfied?"

"Not yet, "he said and looked at my crotch. "But I'm getting there. Sorry about all that. I have a lot of enemies. One can't be too careful." He turned his back to me and headed towards the kitchen. "Now about that drink. What's your pleasure?"

I thought about the plan. Get him to loosen up. Get a confession and then call in Bunn, Larson, and the rest of the cavalry. But after looking at his smug face and thinking about Denise, I couldn't hold back my rage.

I grabbed a vase and smashed it over his head. The crash was like symbols. He staggered a bit but didn't fall. That's when I knew I had to move fast. So I jumped on this massive back like a WWE wrestler. I used my forearm to choke the shit out of 'em. "This is for Denise, motherfucker," I said into his ear with my teeth clenched.

His adrenaline took over because the next thing I knew, I was flying through the air like I had a pilot's license. Within seconds, I was staring at the ceiling and my back felt like it had been split up the middle. When I searched for Prince, he was yanking the cord from a lamp that sat on an end table. I rolled to the kitchen area. Grunted as I stood to my feet and picked up a chair. Now he was facing me and looking pissed.

Thwack!

I wacked him in his dome with the chair and the lamp fell to the floor. He fell backwards over the back of the sofa. I checked the door to make sure the towers weren't coming.

I dove on him. Put my hands around his neck again. Fuck the confession, I thought. I just wanted his ass to die.

He didn't.

Prince used his bear paws to break my stranglehold. Made a fist the size of Toledo and hit my head into a state of I-don't-know-who-the-fuck-I-am-ness. From the eye I could still see out of, I saw Prince smiling.

"Ain't this some shit?" he said. Even sounded like a man again. "I come in here expecting a good time and I end up fighting off a dumb ass, love struck nigga like you."

"Love struck?" I said to throw him off. "What the fuck you talkin' 'bout?"

"Don't try to play me. This is for Denise," he sang in a high-pitch voice meant to mock me. "You damn sure ain't Atlanta PD. I own them motherfuckers. And I know you ain't FBI. They might go deep undercover but deep into some pussy undercover is not in their operations manual."

By now my whole body ached. My head felt like only half of it was working and it was dying. My back throbbed way beyond anything Excedrin could fix. And Prince just kept yapping.

"So that leaves the left behind boyfriend. Am I right?" he asked. I said nothing. "Oh now you don't have shit to say, huh?" Prince laughed. "I gotta admit it Stunner. You got some big ass balls coming in here like this. And for some revenge shit, too."

"Fuck you!" I yelled.

"Not yet baby. That comes later," he said. Androgynous bitch sounded like a woman again too. Then he kissed me on the cheek. I wanted to kill the motherfucker.

"Let me tell you the same thing I told that stank girlfriend of yours when I found her rummaging through my personal files. How the hell a porn chick gonna all of a sudden get some morals over a little under aged sex? A curious bitch can be a dead bitch just like that." He snapped his fingers when he said that.

"You didn't have to kill her, Prince."

"Oh that's where you're wrong, lover boy. I did have to kill her. 'Cause I ain't going to no federal prison for no damn body over some bullshit kiddie porn charges. Not for her, not for the chief of police, and not for you."

Prince limped into the kitchen and grabbed a butcher knife. I used everything in me to try to move off the floor but the pain was too much.

He returned and sat on the sofa I had knocked him over. All the while, I was thinking, *Protect your cornhole, Ricky.*

"You know, I made a mistake when I said you have big balls coming up in here. What I should have said was *had* big balls. Now take off your goddamn pants!"

My heart was doing double-time. The words had me pissed from my head to my toes. And that's when something triggered my brain. In a split second, I could feel my toes wiggle in my shoe. Then my foot felt like it was working again. Next thing you know, my leg was working, too. If I focused all my energy, I could muster up a strong kick and get that knife out of his hands.

"I can't move."

"Oh, do you need a little help?" He moved from the couch and leaned over me. Held the knife in a fist, started undoing my pants button and zipper with the other. "I'm gonna fuck you like the bitch that you are," he said. "Then I'm going to keep your balls as a souvenir."

Now I wished I'd taken Luther up on that bear trap contraption. I wanted to kick his ass. Or at least muster up the strength to kick. I focused all of my energy on waking up my leg. I knew it worked because I felt it in my thigh, my knee, and then my ankles and toes.

Dumb motherfucker didn't even see it take flight towards his head.

Prince was out cold on the floor. The butcher knife lay beside him.

"Did you guys get all that?" I said into the wire. It made me look like a fool as if I was talking to my dick and expecting an answer.

"Roger that. We are en route," Larson said.

I fell on my knees beside him around the same time I heard the sirens. Then I picked up the knife.

I'd like to say that's how it ended. How I had Prince's confession on tape and the sweetest revenge was to have him stand trial and watch as he lost everything and ended up somebody's prison bitch for life in a federal pen. But prison would have been too good for the bastard. So I looked him straight in the face, kneeled over him, and used both my hands to plunge the knife straight through his cold heart.

The twin towers came bursting through the door. I guessed the sound of sirens made them worry.

"Is everything all right?" the quieter one asked. After the two of them saw the suite all jacked up, blood everywhere, and me kneeling over Prince's dead body, the quiet one drew his weapon.

"I wouldn't do that if I were you. This whole place is wired (At least my nuts were.) and those sirens you hear are the FBI. If I was you, I'd get out of here before they find a reason to lock you up."

It didn't take long for them to think about it. They were out in a flash.

I wondered why they hadn't come earlier when they heard the crashing, grunting, and yelling. Probably thought it was some manly sex going on up in there.

I thought about the fallout with Ari and Mike. I'd lost a lot for this shit. And even after the fight, the statement to Bunn and Larson and the other Feds, and after the paramedics carted Prince's lifeless body away, I still was empty. Denise was still gone forever and nothing was going to change that.

Chapter 24

I arrived at Hartsfield Jackson International the next afternoon bruised and battered. My first stop was the cemetery where Denise was buried. Had my dad been with me, he would have told me I was wasting my time. He believed there was no point in talking to dead bodies because the soul had already moved on to its final destination. But I felt a visit was appropriate.

It was bright and sunny but not burn-your-ass hot like Vegas. As I viewed the marble headstone that bared her name, year of birth and death, I felt the need to talk to her.

"Hey, Denise baby. It's me Ricky. I sure do miss you. I miss how we had our morning talks at the kitchen table before we went to work. I miss that snort of yours when you laughed at my jokes. And I really miss kissing every inch of your body from when we used to make love."

I wiped some dust off her gravestone. Looked around to see if anyone was near. There was an elderly woman about half a football field away, putting flowers on a grave. Other than her, it was empty. I continued.

"Denise, I know what Stacy Prince did to you. Knowing you, you probably would have told me to forgive him and just move on. But you know me, I

ain't the forgiving kind. I got him for you, baby.
Perverted ass bastard. Sent his ass straight to hell.
And who knows? Maybe there will be a relative or a
crony coming after me to get revenge. Worst case
scenario, I end up right with you. And that ain't so
bad. But no matter what, you'll always be right
here," I said as I patted my heart. "I love you,
baby."

As I turned to leave, I saw Melissa making her
way towards me with flowers in hand. She was a
good distance away, way farther than earshot. When
she looked up and saw me, she froze for a few
seconds. Then I started walking towards her. She
smiled and walked towards me.

"Melissa, what are you doing here?"

"I figured it was time I paid my respects to
Denise. I didn't mean to interrupt."

"No, it's okay. I was just leaving."

She pursed her lips and nodded. Gave me a
once over and asked, "So what happened to you?"

"Oh. This is nothing," I said as a looked at the
bandages. "You should see the other guy." She
wrinkled her forehead but offered nothing else.

"So did you hear about Monte?"

"No. I've been…away. What's up?"

"There was an announcement from the top that
he took a leave of absence. In fact, it was right after
I set up that meeting between the two of you."

"Really?"

"Really. Rumor has it he and his wife are getting divorced. You wouldn't know anything about that would you?"

"Who me? Where did you get an idea like that?"

"I have my sources," she said with assurance. "Well anyway, guess who's going to be directing features while he's gone?"

"Um, Sugar Tits McGee?"

She punched me on the arm like a schoolgirl. "Very funny."

"I'm just kidding. I guess congrats are in order."

"Congrats accepted. And if you ever decide you want to get in this business for real, I could use a guy with your skills."

"Thanks Melissa, but my adult film making days are over."

"Over before they even started. That's a shame," she said. Bit her bottom lip.

"Let me ask you this, Melissa. If you and Denise were friends, why weren't you at her funeral?"

"Are you kidding? Monte told us all that we were strictly forbidden from attending. Said he was told from the top that anyone seen there would be fired. Like I always say, a girl's gotta eat."

I guess that made sense.

"Oh, okay. Well look," I said. I glanced at my watch. "I really need to jet. Maybe I'll see you around Atlanta some time."

"I'd like that."

Chapter 25

It was a cool, November morning in Atlanta. The shit with the Phone Room was a done deal. I didn't have the energy to fight Mike and Ari in court. Plus Denise's name had been dragged through the mud enough already. I took the settlement and left it at that. I could always start over if I wanted to.

My bags were packed for a three-month stay with an old military buddy when I got a knock at my door. A peek out the window revealed two familiar faces. I opened the door.

"Well if it isn't Bunn and Larson."

"Ricky Stunt," Larson said. "Good to see you. May we come in?"

"Sure."

The agents made themselves comfortable on my sofa.

"How's everything been man? It's been a few months." Bunn said.

"It was kind of rough before but it's getting better. With that bastard Prince dead and those dirty cops facing trials, I at least have some closure."

Larson looked at my wounds. "I see you're getting all healed up."

"You can't keep a good man down. You know that."

"Now what's this I hear about you going to Italy?" Larson asked.

"Man, nothing gets past you guys. A man can't even take a vacation. I'll bet if I told you I took a shit last night you'd tell me what color it was."

We all laughed.

"Nah. Nothing like that. Turns out our boss knows your buddy. They got to talking and…"

"…And so much for my vacation from it all."

"Relax. We want you to have a great vacation. No one deserves it more," Bunn said.

"No one," Larson added.

"Plus, we know you lost your business because of everything that went down."

"Wait. Hold up. Why are you guys really here?"

"All right, Stunt. We'll level with you. There's this case over in Venice. Scumbags involved in human trafficking, kidnapped some underage American girls. Our agents can't get anywhere near it. And since you're going to be right in Aviano visiting your old buddy, we thought you might want to poke around."

"Poke around, huh? And what's in it for me?"

"The Bureau is willing to pay you pretty handsomely as a consultant. And if you can help us out like I know you can, we could put in a good word on making you a regular agent."

"Regular agent? After a Dishonorable Discharge? I don't think so."

"Right. Well, at least the consultant part."

"I'll think about it. Damn. A man can't even take a vacation around here."

"Just thought you'd be interested in making a little money. Plus, let's face it; you were born for this shit," Larson said.

If I did it, it wouldn't be about the money. I had my savings, the one hundred grand from the settlement with Ari and Mike, and another twenty grand from my short but adventurous film career.

"Let me think about it."

"That's good enough for me," Larson said.

Epilogue

Three months later on a cold winter night in Atlanta, Ari's wife promised they'd do something special to celebrate their anniversary. The kids were at a sleepover so it was just the two of them that night. He had been working harder as the new CEO of The Phone Room and thought he deserved a night of excitement with his wife.

As he sat up in bed wearing nothing but his boxers, laptop on his lap, he went over the financials one more time. With that horndog Ricky Stunt out of the way, he could focus on making this a billion-dollar company. Even though there was a newly-appointed CFO in place, he couldn't help but go over the numbers himself. He loved the money part of the business. And like they say, you can take the man out of the numbers game but you can't take the numbers game out of the man.

Fran emerged from the bathroom wearing a silky, pink negligee that went down to her ankles. She also wore a big smile. For a woman close to 50, she still had enough cuteness and even sexiness to keep Ari faithful.

"Happy anniversary," she said to him as she joined him in bed.

"Happy anniversary to you too, dear." They punctuated the statements with a long, dry kiss.

"I have a surprise for you," she said.

"OK. Should I close my eyes?"

"No, sweetheart," she said as she got the DVD remote. "You definitely want to keep your eyes open for this." She didn't have a clue.

The blue light from the flat screen filled the room as it displayed the words:

BUCK NEKKID PRODUCTIONS PRESENTS...

THE AUDACITY OF HOES

"Aren't *we* being a little kinky tonight," he said with excitement.

"I figured we might do something to spice things up tonight."

"I like where this is going," he said. Then he began to remove the negligee while showering her with kisses. Ari peeked up at the TV screen to witness the action.

Imagine Ari's shock as he watched Ricky Stunt using his huge black cock to bang the hell out of some big-breasted bimbo.

Book Club Suggested Discussion Questions

What is your opinion of Ricky Stunt?

Do you believe it is possible to fall in love with an ex-porn star?

Who did you suspect was Denise's killer?

How did you feel about the sex scenes in this book?

Have you ever worked with anyone like Ari?

Why do you think Mike turned against Ricky?

Did you think Ricky would have sex with Stacy Prince?

What was your overall opinion of the book?

What do you think of Jet Black as a writer?

Would you read the sequel "6 to Midnight," previewed in this book?

Six to Midnight

Chapter 1

As I sat on the plane before takeoff to Italy, all kinds of things ran through my head. I was finally getting over Denise's death and was satisfied that the person responsible for it paid dearly. I thought about what my parents would do if they ever found out about that lifestyle and the things I had to do just to find my fiancé's killer.

Nowadays, if anybody mentions Venus Versus Mars, I can't help but to replace the word "venus" with "anus." And of course, that takes me right back to that shit-kicker and shit-eater Vivian and my pukefest. Not to mention my short-lived undercover porn career.

And who would have thought that after chasing me all through Atlanta that Bunn and Larson would not only end up as allies but help me get this contracted gig I was headed to? Not that I have any particular experience in kidnapping cases.

I figured the world must be going crazy with its fetishes and kiddie porn and now sex slaves. It made me almost wish for the ho-hum life of running a telemarketing company again. Prospects and customers might cuss you out or take their money elsewhere but at least you didn't have to wash your crotch three times after you're done with work.

And that Melissa. I can't believe she was trying to make me the next John Holmes *and* get her freak on with me at the same time. What was she thinking?

"Would you like something to drink," the soft voice asked snapping me out of my thoughts. Baby girl was fine too. Reminded me of Nicole Ari-Parker in her *The Incredibly True Adventure of Two Girls in Love*-days. Though this flight attendant had hair down to her shoulders. Her Delta Airlines uniform was a tight Christmas package just waiting to be unwrapped.

"Sure. Scotch and soda."

Our eyes connected for a lot longer than they should have. Her stare suggested that she was interested in serving me more than just some minis and peanuts.

"Do I know you? You look awfully familiar."

Oh shit. Had it started? Maybe the DVD had gone viral. She probably gathered around the computer with her flight attendant buddies and watched *The Audacity of Hoes* on YouTube. I knew I should have never agreed to let them film my face. Should've just stuck to the stunt dick routine and left it at that.

"Whoa," she said after noticing the tension in my face. "It was just a cheesy line."

"A cheesy line?"

220

"Yeah. You know like you so fine I'd drink a tub of yo' bath water."

The geriatric woman with gray hair seated by the window in my row looked up from her magazine and smiled at us.

"Sorry. Didn't mean to cause a scene or anything."

"Pulease. I'm from da hood. Detroit represent," she said like a joke.

"Detroit? For real? Get out of here. I'm from the D too."

"What high school?"

"Renaissance."

"Cass Tech," she said with pep.

Just then we heard a ding followed by the flashing light nine rows up. She sucked her teeth. "Well, duty calls. I'll be back in a few with your scotch and soda. By the way, I'm Nicole."

What are the odds? I thought to myself.

"Ricky," I said. "I look forward to it."

***

"It's kind of tight in here," I said after I closed the bathroom door behind me. It felt like the walls would close in on us.

"There's plenty of room for what I'm about to do to you," she said as she swooped in for a kiss. With her tongue in my mouth and her hands on my ass, I dropped the note in my hands that read:

WANNA JOIN THE MILE-HIGH CLUB
MEET ME IN THE RESTROOM IN 5 MINUTES.
---Nicole

She unbuttoned my shirt in a flash as I started working on pulling down her pantyhose. I put my hand under her blue skirt and was pleased to discover there were no panties serving as a fortress between my fingers and her wetness.

With my shirt unbuttoned, she kissed on my chest and made my belt buckle jingle. I took my free hand and helped her out. Unzipped my pants and let my cock out to stand proud. Then she hiked her skirt up to her stomach. She started unbuttoning her blouse before sitting on the itty bitty sink. Without further ado, I took my hand from her pussy and rubbed the juice on my dick. It was now pointing due North.

"Do you have a condom?" she asked. And for a minute, I had to remember that this is the real world. No flashing lights. No director telling me where to jizz. No 24-hour HIV test. And nobody like Melissa to vouch for me that I'm clean.

"And what if I said no?"

"Then I won't be able to redeem your Mile High Club rewards points."

We laughed. Then I reached into my pocket and found my wallet. I'd packed a couple of Magnums just for such an occasion. I ripped it out and rolled it on. She lifted up her pink bra and

revealed some of the most bodacious Tah Tahs I'd
ever seen.

"You like that?" she asked.

"Me likey."

I eased my dick into her inch by inch to see
how much she could take. I hadn't even put it all the
way in yet when I saw her eyes grow wide.

"It's kind of tight in here," I said as her walls
closed in on me.

"Oh baby. Yeah!" She shouted like this wasn't
a public restroom on an airplane. Some unlucky
bastard in the worst seat on the plane was probably
hearing a free show.

I put my index finger over my lips to shush her
but the smell of her pussy on my hand made me
want to fuck her even harder. So I covered her
mouth with my hand and gave her the full eight.

In and out. Out and in. Banging her head up
against the mirror. Her muffled yells made my hand
vibrate. Her eyes started to water.

Her titties looked lonely so I played with them
with my other hand. Back and forth. Pinching the
nipples and watching them grow.

I put my tongue in her mouth. Sucked her
tongue. It tasted minty and wet. Now I had two
hands free to play with those perky little breasts
while I jack-hammered my pelvis fast and strong.

She closed her eyes like she was in some euphoric trance listening to Sander Van Doorn and hopped up on Ecstasy.

I needed those succulent breasts in my mouth so I stopped kissing her and put the wet hand over her mouth. Then I licked around the nipples and sucked them in before trying to get each breast fully into my mouth.

Nicole dug her nails into my skin, which was a turn on all by itself. And when I looked up, she already had that familiar look on her face that I knew oh too well. This was a meeting in the ladies' room and she was about to climax.

Boom. Boom. Boom. Someone was knocking on the door.

Oh shit. We were busted.

"Go away," she yelled.

We listened as I kept stroking. Finally, we heard the footsteps do as they were told. As I thunder-pumped harder, she whispered in my ear, "Oh Ricky. I'm about to cum."

I smiled and gave myself an imaginary pat on the back.

"Cum with me."

"Okay."

I closed my eyes and pumped. Harder. Faster. Nice rhythm like a Tiesto song was playing in the background. In and out. Circles. Clockwise. Counter-clockwise. North. South. East. West. I

224

palmed her boobs for leverage. Plus they were too damn sexy to leave unattended to.

She oohed and aahhed like after the edits of Anus Versus Mars after the voiceovers. Held on to me for dear life like the rollercoaster was at the top of the hill and about to descend.

Nicole grabbed my head, looked me in the eyes, and yelled loud enough for the cockpit to hear, "I'm cumming!"

Fuck it, I thought. Felt my load making its way to its final destination.

"I'm cumming, too!"

A few minutes later, I came down from the high and we started to get dressed. Then the banging on the door started again.

"A couple of minutes," she said. Then she let out a happy but tired smile like she'd just finished a marathon. She shook her head at me and laughed.

"You really are something else, Mister Ricky Stunt," she said as clasps and buttons were done and nakedness was no more.

"Thanks. You're not so bad yourself. And how do you know my last name is Stunt? I never told you that."

"You really don't remember me, do you?" she asked as she checked her makeup and washed away smudged lipstick.

"Should I?"

"I'll give you a clue. You took my sister's virginity in the back of a Chevy."

I looked at her again. This time, I really studied her face and saw it. "Oh my god. You're Shakita's little sister. Little Nicki."

"Not so little anymore."

"You had to be like ten years old when I fuc…I mean, when I was with your sister."

"If you could see the look on your face right now. Don't worry, Ricky. I'm a grown-ass woman now. And ooh wee," she said while grabbing my crotch, "my sister was right about you. You got some skills." Nicole opened the door.

As if that surprise wasn't enough, imagine how I felt when I saw the puzzled look on the little boy's face as Nicole and I emerged from the restroom together. She looked at the boy, then at me and busted out laughing.